IT WAS WHITE, THIS FIGURE

White streaked with black, like the atmosphere of Gehenna herself. Its outlines were fuzzy, threatening to dissolve at any moment back into the surrounding mists. I became aware of the voices ringing in my ears once again, the very same sirens which had called to me in my dreams. But this time I was fully awake.

The voices increased in force. *Join us,* they seemed to say. *Embrace us. Join us, as the other man has already done.*

I felt a mixture of desire and terror. I wanted to roll in the soft and yielding moss, to breathe the sweet air of this planet, to live out my dreams. At the same time, I wanted to scream.

Terror won. I did scream, again and again.

"Intense...burning like a trail of gunpowder from the first page to the last."

—Roger Zelazny

ISAAC ASIMOV PRESENTS

STATION GEHENNA

ANDREW WEINER

WORLDWIDE®

TORONTO • NEW YORK • LONDON • PARIS
AMSTERDAM • STOCKHOLM • HAMBURG
ATHENS • MILAN • TOKYO • SYDNEY

For my father, Joseph Weiner,
and for my mother, Raie Weiner.

With thanks to Richard Curtis,
Gardner Dozois, Terence M. Green
and Barbara Moses.

STATION GEHENNA

A Worldwide Library Book/Decemb 1988

ISBN 0-373-30306-8

First published by Congdon & Weed, Inc.

Parts of this work have appeared, in slightly different form,
in *The Magazine of Fantasy and Science Fiction*.

Science Fiction Mysteries

by Isaac Asimov

Mysteries and science fiction are two branches of literature that did not become possible, in their modern sense, until human society had developed to some appropriate pitch.

Thus, you couldn't very well write mysteries until society had developed organized police forces to combat crime. Until then the occasional crime-detection story was enjoyed but these were few and out of the ordinary.

Again, you couldn't very well write science fiction until society had developed science and technology to the point where change was fast enough to be visible and the notion of an advanced future began to make sense. Until then, the occasional fanciful story was enjoyed but these were few and out of the ordinary.

It follows that the modern story and the modern science fiction story both date back to the early nineteenth century and, as it happens, each received its most important early impulse from the writings of one man—Edgar Allan Poe.

In other respects, though, the two genres are different, even antithetical.

The mystery story represents the triumph of order. Crime (particularly murder) upsets the social fabric. It introduces an element of anarchy. Someone has deliberately deviated from the accepted code of social behavior to seek some sort of satisfaction through unsanctioned methods.

Presumably such an action, however small in itself, threatens us all, since if it is uncorrected, unpunished, and unavenged, it will open the door for further such actions and end by destroying society.

The protagonist of the story then must discover the nature of the anarchic action, the circumstances, the individual or individuals who attempted the perversion of society. He must reveal the culprit and bring about his punishment. Order is restored and the social fabric is saved, so that the story ends exactly where it began.

The science fiction story, however, represents the triumph

of disorder. A science fiction story must be set against a society significantly different from our own—usually, but not necessarily, because of some change in the level of science and technology—or it is not a science fiction story.

This means that, to begin with, the science fiction story destroys our own comfortable society. The science fiction story does not deal with the restoration of order, but with change and, ideally, with continuing change. In the science fiction story, we leave our society and never return to it.

In fact, if we were to return to our society, if order were to be restored, the science fiction story would be a flat failure. Imagine a science fiction story in which the nuclear bomb is invented, in which its dangers are recognized, and in which the hero succeeds in suppressing the knowledge so that everything continues as before. That is not the way things work. When Pandora's box is opened, then, whether for good or evil, the world changes. The science fiction writer may seek for solutions and even find them, but the one forbidden solution is that of forcing everything back into the box.

Can there then be a fusion of these two types of story—that of quintessential order and that of quintessential disorder? To be sure, mysteries can be written in which science plays a factor. Arthur Conan Doyle wrote of Sherlock Holmes, a scientific detective who was always peering through his magnifying glass at bits of tobacco ash. R. Austin Freeman's Dr. Thorndyke is an even better example of the scientific detective, and scientific minutiae often play a role in the mystery stories of the classic type.

In the same way, science fiction stories often have a mystery motif, as in Lewis Padgett's *Private Eye* or Alfred Bester's *The Demolished Man*. Usually, though, the science fiction is totally dominant, and the mystery would not stand on its own.

John W. Campbell, Jr., science fiction's greatest editor, maintained that a perfect fusion was impossible. In 1953, to show him wrong, I wrote *The Caves of Steel*, a science fiction mystery in which each element is equally strong, and in which each supports the other. I then wrote *The Naked Sun* and *The Robots of Dawn* as sequels just to show that the first was no accident.

I am not the only one who does it, and here is Andrew Weiner's *Station Gehenna* to demonstrate that.

1

The captain of the ship, a morose individual in his middle years, accompanied me to the launch bay to give me a formal send-off. It was the appropriate thing for him to do, of course, given my rank and stature within the company, but the captain had demonstrated little prior interest in such formalities. Indeed, we had exchanged hardly a dozen words in the course of the month-long run out to Gehenna, sitting through meal after meal at his table in the galley in an increasingly strained silence.

"This is it," he said. "This is as far as we go."

His tone was neither regretful nor apologetic. It betrayed, if anything, a definite eagerness to be rid of me, to deposit me as quickly as possible like the excess baggage he so obviously perceived me to be. For my own part, I was as anxious to be on my way as he was to see me go.

The hostile attitude of the ship's crew, of whom the captain was entirely typical, was hardly a new experience for me. I had been through exactly the same thing time and time again, and I was far too much of a professional to allow myself to be really bothered by it. I had long ago learned how to put my splendid isolation to good use, lying on my bunk for hours at a time catching up on the professional literature or meditating on the mission that lay ahead.

Yet all the same, it grew wearisome after awhile. And a month was a long time to spend under such conditions—the longest voyage I had ever been required to undertake. I was bored with inaction, anxious to move ahead with what promised to be the most important and demanding mission of my career.

The captain made a tentative, oddly jerky motion with his right hand, as though reaching out to shake the gross metallic paw of my atmosphere suit. If that was his original notion, he quickly thought better of it and instead began to tug at the hem of his jacket, as if this was what he had intended all along.

His awkwardness signalled to me a certain nervousness, at once quite understandable and utterly misplaced. The captain believed he had something to fear from me. He was well aware, after all, that I was a psychologist attached to the investigative field services group of our mutual employer, R. G. Spooner Interplanetary Development Corporation. And, as a highly trained professional, I could hardly have failed to note the poor mental health of this vessel's crew, including that of the captain himself.

But I had no brief to report on the captain or his crew. And the company, in any event, had always granted a certain leeway in what was considered to be acceptable behavior on the part of space-going personnel. They are, in many respects, a very special breed of person, and this has always been reflected in our recruitment and selection procedures.

"Well," I said. "Be seeing you."

He nodded. This same ship was scheduled to pick me up in three months, on the return leg of its voyage. He did not seem overjoyed at that prospect.

And then the captain dismissed me, abruptly, from his field of vision, turning to stare down gloomily through the viewing port to the dreadful face of the planet below. I followed his gaze for a moment, taking in the sight, a grubby whitish murk scarred by darker patches, then quickly looked away.

Gehenna. I had first caught sight of it earlier that day, watching from the observation deck as the ship burst out of the null and into the real. It was then only a tiny disk, from a distance no more menacing than the moon seen from Earth, but as we raced closer I had been able to see it in its full and repellent splendor. It was, I had thought then, an unlikely enough habitat for humanity. But such indeed it would be.

I sealed the faceplate of my suit and clumped over to the landing vehicle. A crewman opened up the hatch for me. From the darkness inside, I could see the dials on the instrument panel glowing faintly.

"The station's beacon will guide you down," the crewman told me. "There's no need to worry about any of that." He indicated the control panel. "So just relax and take it easy and you'll be as snug as a pea in a pod."

I nodded, accepting this somewhat patronizing explanation without comment. I had probably spent many more hours locked up in these flying tin cans than had the crewman. I lowered myself into the cramped interior of the vehicle.

As snug as a pea in a pod. Space travelling personnel, as I well knew, often referred to this type of one-person lander as a "pod." Although myself no novice to these journeyings, I personally detested the term. I have always resisted the tendency to project these needless anthropomorphisms upon the machinery of our own device.

The crewman closed the hatch over my head. Now the darkness was complete, but for the flicker of dials on the control panel, bearing information that could not possibly concern me. As the crewman had observed, the lander was fully automated, launched by the ship and guided down by the signal of the receiving facility below. This sequence would take place without deviation, or else the vehicle would crash and I would die. I could not affect the outcome in either case.

A short-run vehicle, it was not designed for creature comfort. Crouched down inside there in the darkness, I felt an all-too-familiar unease. Far from that of a pea comfortably nestling in its pod, the experience had always seemed to me more akin to that of some sardine packed inside a can. However you looked at it, it was a loss of control, a situation which always brought out in me a mild yet still disturbing anxiety.

A pea in a pod, a sardine in a can. I racked my brains for a more appealing image. Perhaps, I thought, I was like a child in the womb, floating comfortably in warmth and safety, waiting for birth.

Waiting, that is, to plunge helplessly into an unfamiliar and unremittingly hostile world.

Irritated with myself, I tried to focus my thoughts on the situation I would be facing at Station Gehenna. It would be a difficult one, no doubt, and likely to challenge my abilities to the fullest. But it would not, finally, prove impenetrable, once attacked with efficiency and rationality, the very qualities upon which I had built my so-far successful career.

On this score I was wrong. But of course I did not know that as the falling began, the falling of that darkened tin can into the appalling white murk below.

The falling to Gehenna.

2

The motion of the landing vehicle ceased with a slight jolt. The hatch began to roll back automatically. Immediately, whitish fumes rushed into the vehicle, a first taste of the noxious atmosphere of Gehenna. It was composed, according to my briefings, of water vapor, carbon dioxide, methane, ammonia, and assorted ambient hydrocarbons, along with a small but steadily growing proportion of oxygen.

Grasping my single bag, I wriggled out through the hatch and climbed down to the floor of the receiving bay. The ceiling was sliding back into place above my head. I took bearings on the exit lock leading into the station proper and began to shuffle in that direction.

There was a shudder as the pumps started up their work of expelling the invading atmosphere back into the world outside the station. In another fifteen years, I had learned from the briefing documents, such work would become unnecessary. By then this station would have completed its program, which was nothing less than the complete transformation of the Gehennan biosphere. By then the air outside the station would approximate Earth normal, permitting easy colonization and easy access to this planet's considerable mineral wealth.

There had initially been some debate within the company, I had been told, as to the cost-effectiveness and general advisability of this development plan. Some elements within the senior management group had argued for a cheaper and less sweeping terraforming program. They had suggested that a little tinkering with the climate, leaving the atmosphere much as it was, would have been quite sufficient here. It would have permitted the easy operation of automated equipment controlled by a handful of humans living in climate-controlled conditions, as had been the model in earlier local system planetary developments.

Others had argued for bypassing Gehenna altogether, for accelerating existing development programs or for pushing on toward more welcoming habitats.

But these debates had come to an abrupt halt when the founder and chairman of the company, the great R. G. Spooner himself, had declared himself in favor of the maximum terraforming option.

"We go all the way," he had said in his clip for the employee newsvid, tugging vigorously at his long white beard with his left hand. That was the mechanical one, of course, the one which had replaced the hand he lost so many years ago on some frontier planet far away. Much better mechanicals were available today, virtually indistinguishable from the real thing, while doctors had in recent years been scoring impressive successes with limb transplants. But Spooner still wore that old mechanical hand, pitted and rusty now, like some sort of campaign badge.

"To accept anything less," he had said, "would be to admit defeat."

Always an imposing figure, Spooner seemed to grow wilder and more powerful with each passing year, until he bestrode the entire planet like the colossus he was, a prophet of almost biblical intensity and ferocity of a new age for humanity. Neither Spooner nor his works were to everyone's taste, but I personally admired him tremendously. I admired that overweening sense of destiny, that fierce and almost mystical drive to control nature in all its forms, which had allowed him to build the largest and most successful corporation the world had ever known.

That corporation had changed a great deal in character, of course, since its pioneering days. Spooner's impulsive and inspiring yet occasionally reckless leadership had been tempered by the advent of a cadre of more professional managers who had increasingly taken command of its day-to-day operations. Yet when Spooner made a decision, as he did so infrequently these days, it would be carried out.

And so the company had proceeded with the maximum terraforming option on Gehenna. It was the most ambitious of all the company's herculean planetary development efforts, a multi-billion-dollar roll of the dice that would tie up the greater part of its working capital and borrowing abilities for at least a decade to come.

And yet, imposing though he was, not even Spooner could entirely deny the ravages of time. The great man was in his eighties now, his attention was known to wander, and his health was not much better than could be expected. And his voting control over the company had been progressively diffused among his children for purposes of estate and succession planning. None of these heirs openly opposed him, but it was said that some whispered of his folly and waited eagerly for him to stumble.

The transformation of Gehenna was so far proceeding according to plan. And yet there was now at least a hint of doubt as to whether this plan could be completed. It was this doubt I had come to Station Gehenna to resolve. In a sense, then, the whole future of this planet, along with the ongoing viability of the company in terms of recouping on its considerable capital investment here, rested upon my shoulders. It was a burden I had accepted enthusiastically.

Station Gehenna was the company's prime terraforming facility, the key link in a chain of ten such facilities spread out across the face of this planet. It was also the only inhabited site of the entire planet, providing shelter for the handful of personnel who monitored the progress of the effort and serviced, as required, the automated substations.

Technical problems had so far been few. The personnel, rather than their machines, were providing the element of doubt as to the future of this project. It was they who accounted for my presence here.

The light over the lock flashed green and the door swung back to welcome me. I stepped through into a smaller chamber. Sensors triggered the door to close behind me. Jets of cleansers flushed clean my atmosphere suit and my hand luggage.

It reminded me somehow of going to the carwash with my father, one of our few common interests during my childhood. Privately owned automobiles were few and far between these days, and it was a long time since I had been in a carwash.

Another light flickered on, and I was able to step through into the interior of the station, raising my faceplate as I went, nerving myself for the masquerade to come.

There was a welcoming party of one, a slight, dark, nervous-looking young man with restless, darting eyes. I recognized him from my briefings as techperson Norman Remus.

"Commander Muller sends his regards," Remus said. "He asked me to show you to your living quarters."

I gathered from his tone that this was not an assignment he had accepted with any great enthusiasm.

"I'm Norm Remus. Techperson."

He stepped forward to help me climb out of my bulky atmosphere suit.

"Leisure officer Victor Lewin," I said.

The masquerade had begun.

3

"So you're going out again?" Rosemary had asked after I had dropped off Jesse.

I had told Jesse as much the week before, but Rosemary had made no mention of it when I had picked him up for the weekend. She had been in a hurry to meet her current lover, an assistant philosophy professor. Jesse did not like him, but then, he had never demonstrated much enthusiasm for any of the lovers she had taken in the five years since our separation. Not even for Phil, who had lasted by far the longest, and who had taken him to innumerable baseball games, something I had rarely had the fortitude to do.

"Yes," I said. "Next week."

"How long this time?"

"Almost half a solar," I said.

"Is that months or years?" she asked. "I never could get that straight."

"Years," I said. "It means Earth-years. You know that."

"It's easier to ask," she said, "than to have to clutter up my mind remembering things like that."

She affected a yawn. Rosemary had always been a great believer in economy of intellectual effort. Some might have thought this a surprising trait in a university teacher, although I knew better. The universities were no longer attracting our best, indeed they showed no signs of wishing to attract them, and my own brief career in academia was a case in point. My colleagues, resenting my productivity and originality, had ultimately denied me a tenured position, whereas Rosemary's colleagues had embraced her, precisely because she was exactly like them.

"Half a solar, then," she said. "That's a long one. It must be very far indeed."

"Yes," I said. "Very far away. Practically the perimeter."

"Where there are no boundaries," she said.

Presumably this was some sort of allusion. Rosemary was very big on allusions. It was part of her stock-in-trade as a popcult historian.

When I had first met Rosemary, I had thought her choice of academic specialty to be an expression of some inner humor and whimsy. Later I realized that what appealed to her for the most part was the simplicity of the material, its ease of manipulation. *Death and dying in the songs of Leonard Cohen. Deconstructing Grodd: crime and punishment in mid-period Flash. Gay deceivers: hidden homosexuality in the English detective novel.* And so on.

"Well," she said, again. "That is a long time."

There was, I realized, a nagging familiarity to this conversation. How far? How long? When? So many of our discussions had once centered on these questions. The difference was that they had then generated much greater emotional heat, at least in the beginning. Toward the end Rosemary had clearly looked forward to my absences. Now, presumably, they were a matter of indifference to her.

"Yes," I agreed. "Quite long."

"Jesse will miss you," she said.

It was nice of her to say so, but I didn't believe it. Jesse hardly knew me. I had been separated from Rosemary since he was two. Even before that, my job had not allowed me to spend much time with him.

"Well," she said, "have a good trip."

She crossed to the den to make a show of checking on Jesse, who was watching the wallscreen with rapt attention. I did not really approve of him watching the screen to the extent he did, but I was hardly in a position to exert parental authority.

It was my signal to leave, yet for some reason I was reluctant to do so. I could have stood there for hours, in the living room of that cramped but cozy little townhouse, exchanging meaningless and affectless chatter with my ex-wife. I found it oddly pleasurable. It was a bit like coming home.

Not that I had ever lived in this particular house with Rosemary. And not that I harbored any desire for reconciliation. It was Rosemary's life that, momentarily at least, I envied. It was the life I might once have wanted for myself, the life I had indeed once led.

A life, that is, outside the strivings of the managerial classes, yet still elevated economically above the rapidly thinning ranks of the working classes, or the ever-swelling mass of the permanently unemployed, the permies, as we so heartlessly called them and as they had begun to call themselves.

It was not a life that would make you wealthy, yet it had many other redeeming features. Work of at least modest interest and importance. A certain although limited measure of public respect. A sense of collegiality. The opportunity to travel to conferences in interesting places.

And then, of course, there were the short working hours and long vacations, all that time to be filled with amusing academic gossip and pleasurable little affairs.

I could become nostalgic for it even now. And if my application for tenure had been accepted, it was possible that I might still be living that life today, if not with Rosemary then perhaps with a less abrasive version of her. I might never have gone to work for Spooner Interplanetary Development.

It was possible, but it was not terribly likely. The very fact that it had not worked out that way was a good indication that it never could have worked out that way. The academic world had not proved sufficiently large to contain my energies and ambitions. My colleagues had in a sense been perfectly right to deny me tenure. I simply had not fit in.

"Are you staying for dinner?" Rosemary asked, returning from the den.

"I never do."

She nodded, as though that decided the matter. We had come to rely heavily on ritual to guide us through these brief but unavoidable interactions. Perhaps this had been true even during our marriage.

"Am I invited?" I asked, more curious than eager.

"If you like," she said. "But Jill and Ben are coming over."

Jill and Ben Sanders had once been our friends. Both taught at the university, Ben in the same department as Rosemary. I had once had a brief affair with Jill, one year when we were both teaching summer school, and I presumed that at some point Rosemary and Ben had been similarly involved. After the divorce it had become clear that they were Rosemary's friends rather than my own.

As I hesitated Rosemary said, "We're going to look at some old 1980s slasher viddies that Ben has unearthed. We're going to give a presentation at the HPC conference." HPC, as I well knew, was the History of Popular Culture Association, although I felt like asking her for a translation all the same.

The prospect of sitting through a bunch of slasher viddies, and listening to Rosemary and Ben trading allusions, clinched matters, as no doubt she knew it would.

"I think I'll pass," I said. "It might be awkward."

"You're probably right."

She accompanied me to the door.

"I don't understand how you could do it," she said. "I never could understand."

"Do what?"

"Go out there. Go out so far away. Where there are no trees or birds or lakes or even hardly any people. I couldn't do that."

"There are trees, here and there. Trees of a sort. Not where I'm going this time, but there are trees. Lakes, too."

"Don't be so concrete," Rosemary said. "You know what I mean."

"All I'm saying is that it's not as bad out there as you think, most of these places. There's nothing particularly heroic about going out there. A lot of people do it."

"I didn't say it was heroic. I just said that I didn't understand it."

"I didn't say I *liked* it out there. I only said it wasn't so terrible. I go out there because I have to because it's my job to do so. I never said I enjoyed it."

"But you do. Or at least, you like to think that you like it. In any case, I wasn't asking you to defend yourself. I just made an observation."

"I wasn't being defensive. I was just responding to your observation."

"I think we've had this discussion before," she said.

"Yes," I said. "I think we have."

4

Station Gehenna was laid out like a wheel. Corridors radiated out from the center, like spokes. Other corridors, joined by these spokes, formed a series of concentric circles, wheels within the larger wheel. These corridors were clean and well-lit but were painted a somewhat depressing high-gloss green.

My first impression, as I followed Remus toward my quarters, was of the sheer immensity of the place. It could easily have housed a hundred crew members, rather than its much smaller actual personnel complement. As a result it felt, for the most part, empty and echoing, virtually devoid of any sign of human life.

The scale of the place was dictated not by the needs of its inhabitants but by the size of the terraforming equipment. As I walked, I felt a constant humming all around me, as this machinery went about its work.

Remus showed me to my quarters, which were large but only modestly furnished. After I had deposited my single piece of luggage, he accompanied me to the office of the station commander, Franz Muller.

Muller, a big hefty-looking man in his late forties, was sitting behind his desk scowling at a terminal, surrounded by reams of print-outs. He was, by re-

pute, one of the company's best line managers, a vet-
eran of half a dozen development projects, a man with
a reputation for bringing his jobs in on-time and on-
budget. But composing and filing reports would not
be among his interests or strengths.

He looked up as we entered, and stood up to shake
my hand.

"Officer Lewin," he said. "Welcome."

"Pleased to be here," I said.

"That's good," Muller said ponderously, his speech
nearly as ponderous as his bearing. "It's always good
to have a positive outlook."

He nodded to himself, as if in agreement with his
platitude, then seemed at a loss for anything else to
say. His stilted manner only confirmed what I had already learned from his profiles—that he was not at his
best in dealing with people. He was characterized by
an extreme task orientation, a valuable quality under
certain circumstances but perhaps not these.

"Well," I said, finally. "I'm anxious to get started
on assessing staff leisure needs. I was thinking that
perhaps the best approach..."

Muller waved his hand.

"Yes, yes," he said. "By all means. I'm sure you
will keep me informed as to your progress. It's good
to have the services of a leisure officer again, isn't it,
Norm?"

Remus, however, made no attempt even to pretend
to agree with this pleasantry. He just sat there staring
at me.

I decided to take what advantage I could of the
opening which had been presented to me.

"Too bad about Arthur Duggan," I said.

"Oh yes," Muller said heavily. "Too bad. Too bad."

He shook his head mournfully.

I waited expectantly, but he did not seem inclined to elaborate on this statement. Clearly he did not wish to talk about my immediate predecessor in this position of leisure officer, nor the reasons why a replacement was required, just eighteen months into a four-solar tour of duty.

I tried to push the conversation along a little further to see where it might lead.

"He committed suicide, didn't he?" I asked.

Muller nodded, apparently with some reluctance.

"It seems so," he said dully. "I would like to believe it was an accident, but all the signs pointed to suicide, and that's how it was classified in the end."

"I heard that he stepped outside without a protective suit," I said. "That doesn't sound much like an accident."

"I suppose not," Muller said. "It's just so hard to believe that he would do a thing like that."

"Why would he have done it?" I asked. "Was he depressed about his work?"

"Well, yes, perhaps a little. He would complain to me that this place was not conducive to structured recreation. He encountered some resistance." Muller glanced toward Remus. "Toward the end he just seemed to give up. But that's hardly a reason to kill yourself. I imagine it must have been personal. I really don't like to speculate."

"It must have been a very upsetting experience," I said, "for all of you."

"Oh, yes," Muller said. "Very upsetting." He sighed heavily.

"Well, good to meet you, Lewin," he said. "Norm will get you settled in."

The station commander settled back into his report writing. However much he disliked it, he obviously preferred it to talking with me.

5

"Well," Remus told me, as we left Muller's office, "I guess you can find your way back to your quarters. Third-meal is in three hours. The cafeteria is in the inner hub." He gestured vaguely down a corridor. "I have to get back to work."

"I haven't eaten in hours," I said. "Is it possible to get a sandwich or something?"

With apparent reluctance, Remus took me to the station cafeteria, where he introduced me to the nutrition officer.

"Nutrition officer Charlotte McKinley," he said. "This is leisure officer Victor Lewin." And then, almost as an afterthought, "Charlotte is my wife."

I knew this, of course, from the profiles. Remus and McKinley had signed a four-year contract just before their tour of duty had commenced. It was a minimum deal all around, with no joint ownership of property, no children, no covenants for monogamy, no renewal options.

For McKinley, this was both her first marriage and her first tour of duty. Remus had been previously married, to a chemical engineer who had shared his first company posting but declined his offer to renew. Testing revealed that he had been somewhat upset at the time, but he had recovered sufficiently following his remarriage to take on his new posting.

"It's good to have you here," McKinley said, shaking my hand and engaging me in what seemed to be unnecessarily prolonged eye contact as her husband hovered nervously behind me. Finally I looked away. Only then did she smile.

Marital problems, I speculated, synthesizing my intuitive feel for the situation with my prior analysis of their personality profiles.

"Lewin is hungry," Remus told her.

"How about some chicken salad?" she asked. "We synth pretty good chicken here."

She busied herself at her console.

"Well," Remus said, "I should get back to work."

"Yes," she said, "I suppose you should."

After Remus had departed she brought my sandwich and sat down at the mess table with me as I ate it.

"Sorry to be a nuisance," I said.

"No problem," she said. "This is not exactly a demanding job. I was just programming third-meal. When you're finished I'm going to go shut down and watch a vid. We have a pretty good library here."

"What are you watching?"

"This and that. Right now I'm skimming a ten-year run of a classic soapie, *General Hospital*. It helps to pass the time."

Not, I thought, the most fulfilling leisure pursuit, although Rosemary would no doubt have disagreed. Rosemary had written her Ph.D. thesis on ancient and modern soap opera.

Of course, Rosemary was an intellectual, within the most generous definition of that term, while Charlotte McKinley was not. McKinley, I knew, had been recruited by the company straight out of high school and sent on a scholarship to Spooner University. But for her exceptional intelligence, and a higher level of motivation, she was indistinguishable from her classmates, her primary reference group, in norms and values. The company had rescued her from the lifetime on the dole that would otherwise almost certainly have been her fate, as it had been of almost all her classmates.

But for the company, then, she would probably have spent nearly all her time watching vids rather than just some of it. Yet it was a pity that no one had tried to prepare her to make more creative use of her time here. The education provided by Spooner U., while very good on the practicalities, was rather light on everything else.

"You don't approve," she said, obviously reading my expression. "Neither did Arthur."

"Arthur Duggan?"

"He tried to set up this reading program for me, tied into some classic old vids. You know, I would see the vid and then I would read the book. And then we would discuss it."

"It sounds like Arthur Duggan took his work very seriously."

"Oh yes," she said. "Very seriously."

There was something in the way she said this that made me wonder whether she and Arthur Duggan had been lovers.

"We all miss Arthur," she said.

"Well," I said, "I'll do my best to live up to his example. Just let me get settled in and I'll see what I can do in the way of fun and games."

"Fun and games," McKinley said, "is exactly what we need."

6

From the cafeteria I made my way to the rec room to inventory Arthur Duggan's equipment. It would be tedious maintaining this pose, yet I was more convinced than ever that I had chosen the right course. To make a full and proper investigation here I would have to remain incognito, living and working among my unsuspecting subjects.

Charlotte McKinley's account of Arthur Duggan did not exactly square with the picture that emerged from his activity log. Whatever special services he might have rendered to McKinley, he had not for the most part been an especially inventive leisure officer. Nor, toward the end of his life, had he been an especially conscientious one. His log, a rather uninspiring record of bridge games, table tennis tournaments, and mathematical games-playing, petered out into almost nothing in the last six months before his death.

I recalled his suicide note—or at least, what was believed to be a suicide note, a scrap of paper found in his quarters.

"The dreams are intolerable," he had written. *"I can no longer bear the dreams."*

Just that, only that. Little enough to go on.

The table tennis table was thick with dust. I was cleaning it up when I realized that I had a visitor.

"Leisure officer Lewin?" the woman asked. "I'm medical officer Greta Vichevski. I was passing by, so I thought I might introduce myself."

She was a tall, blonde, handsome woman in her early forties. Her smile was warm. A likable person, it seemed, although of course one could not jump to conclusions.

Greta Vichevski had been married to Franz Muller for fourteen years, three contracts, a long time by anyone's standards. And, as I recalled, it was a very strict contract indeed, specifying complete monogamy. No children, of course. One does not raise children in places like Station Gehenna. Apart from anything else, the company would hardly tolerate it. And Vichevski and Muller had been working for the company, in places not unlike this one, for many years.

"I'm glad you're here," she said. "We could all use some diversion."

"From what?"

She gestured vaguely, as if to take in the room, the station, the planet, the universe.

"The monotony," she said. "The monotony gets to you after awhile. Particularly here. Franz and I have served on such stations before, but this may be the worst. Here you cannot even go outside for a walk except in a suit. And then you will see nothing. Only the murk, the filth."

"My predecessor," I said. "Arthur Duggan. I know of course what happened to him. But what do you think made him do it? Could it have been this monotony you speak of that drove him to it?"

She shrugged.

"Most people can handle monotony. It comes with the territory, after all. One does not usually kill oneself out of boredom. Otherwise, we might have a hard time keeping anyone alive out here. As for Arthur Duggan, he went for a walk without his atmosphere suit, and that is really all we know."

"I don't mean to stir up uncomfortable memories," I said. "It's just that the company didn't tell me much about the matter, so naturally I'm a bit curious."

"There's nothing to be curious about, nothing to tell. I knew that he was depressed, of course, but I thought he was no more depressed than any one of us might get from time to time. Perhaps I should have suspected, but I did not. And one day he went for a walk. As to his reasons, I really couldn't say. These things happen, and it's terribly unfortunate. But as Franz says, it's all past history now, and we have to make the best of it."

"Of course," I said, taking this as my cue to drop the subject. "I agree completely."

Yet perhaps Dr. Vichevski did not entirely agree with her husband, for now it was she who pushed the discussion along.

"It's difficult, you know, living so close to one another here. Even in this enormous station. You see the same people every day, have the same conversations, become irritated by the same mannerisms. And you feel the others becoming just as bored and irritated with you. I think we all have a need to go offstage for awhile, now and again, to get away from everyone else. Perhaps that is what Arthur felt, although of course he took matters to extremes. He withdrew from us, and we did not pay as much attention as we should have. And then he went for a walk."

For an amateur, she had a good grasp of the key issues in socio-technical design. Balancing the need for privacy with the need for healthy social interactions was always one of the major challenges facing a small, isolated work group like this one. Of course, that was exactly why the company had sent Arthur Duggan here in the first place.

I tried to respond as a professional leisure officer might respond in the same situation.

"Yes," I said. "I know the problem—I've seen it before many times. And no doubt the death of Arthur Duggan has made things worse rather than better. But there is much that a well-designed leisure program can do to improve matters. Now that I'm here, I'll just have to see what I can do to make you people happier, won't I?"

Perhaps this was not the most sensitive response. Vichevski seemed to grimace at this rather forced note of professional joviality. Or perhaps she was merely weary of the subject.

"I'm sure you will," she said. "In any case, I must be going. I'll see you at third-meal."

She made a rapid exit from the room.

In preparing for this mission I had studied many tapes of leisure experts in the process of social facilitation, and I was doing my best to mimic them. This was not the easiest thing in the world for a person of my temperament and disposition. But I could only try. As Muller had told Vichevski, it was human nature to make the best of things. That was pretty much the key to the human condition, although I myself might not have expressed it so succinctly.

7

"It's a delicate situation," Haines had told me. "Very delicate indeed."

Haines was my immediate superior, manager of the investigative field services group within the company's human resources department. He had once been a field officer like myself, by reputation one of the best, but he had been desk-bound for some years now.

As a manager, he was not inspiring. His supervision was perfunctory at best, except on those occasions when he chose to fuss and nag about the methods his investigators used to get the job done. It was as if he had forgotten everything he had ever learned in the field, forgotten how he had obtained his own results.

Word around the department was that he had plateaued-out, would go no further in the company, would stay at this desk until retirement, unless he was shunted aside first by some brighter and more ambitious contender.

I had some thoughts along those lines myself. One or two more successful interventions and I would surely be in line for promotion. I did not covet Haines's job for itself, but as a stepping stone, a route into the senior levels of the department. From there, perhaps, I might move higher still.

It was no longer ridiculous for a human resources type to aspire to cross over into the chief executive stream. Rather, it appeared to be increasingly the way of the new corporate world.

The current executive vice president of human resources in my own company, for example, was none other than Ronald Spooner, Jr., or Ron Jr., as he was popularly if not always affectionately known to employees.

R.G.'s eldest son, the only one of his children to enter the family firm, was heavily favored to ultimately succeed his father as the company's chief executive officer. If he did so, of course, it would be on the strength of his management skills and personal drive rather than mere nepotism. In the professionally managed organization that R.G. Spooner Interplanetary had become, nothing less would be acceptable.

The very fact that the son of the great pioneer had taken on such a position was evidence enough of its importance. With our current state of technology, managing the money and the machines had become a breeze. It was the people who gave you trouble. We used as few of them as we could, of course, but you had to have some people. And, always, they gave you trouble. As on Gehenna.

"Terrible potential for scandal," Haines had fussed in his most old-womanish way. "Just awful."

It was difficult for me to understand how Haines had ever been able even to function as an investiga-

tive field officer, let alone earn such an impressive
reputation within the company. But the word was that
he had seen something out there, something that had
changed him, and that he was no longer the man he
had once been.

"We've had suicides before," I said. "From time to
time. We've had one or two murders, for that matter.
Nobody made much fuss. Nobody cares that much
about what happens out on these frontier planets."

"Not in the past, no," Haines said. "That's quite
true. But you see, times are changing. We have to be
more sensitive to public attitudes. The company is not
as popular as it might be."

"The company has never been popular."

As the biggest and most aggressive of the dozen or
so interplanetary development companies, R. G.
Spooner had always tended to bear the brunt of public criticism for the great expansion into space. The
labor unions, what remained of them, decried its ex-
port of jobs and capital, its occasional failings in the
area of safety procedures. Environmentalists be-
moaned the destruction of minor and insignificant
alien life forms in the colonization process.

And then there were the Contractionists, a militant
political faction suspected of a number of terrorist
outrages, yet still influential in opinion-forming circles. The Contractionists, a bizarre coalition of fem-
inists, priests, anarchists, nostalgic conservatives, and
other radical debris, opposed all extraterrestrial development activity by the company and its competitors, claiming Earth as the one true temple of the
human spirit.

"Our public affairs specialists perceive further erosion of late," Haines told me. "There is a risk that our activities may become insupportable from the point of view of the governing authorities, no matter how sympathetically disposed they may be toward us."

Here, of course, Haines was referring to the company's not inconsiderable contributions to both the political advancement and personal comfort of those same authorities.

"The Gehenna situation," Haines continued, "is particularly sensitive. As our first true terraforming project, it represents a major test of our credibility and resolve. I'm sure you know that the chairman himself has taken a personal interest in the project."

"I understand the sensitivities involved," I said, although I thought that, as usual, he was exaggerating them. "You can rest assured that I will handle this matter as delicately as possible. I am, after all, one of your most experienced investigators."

I was, in point of fact, his best investigator, perhaps even better than he had been in his prime, and Haines knew it as well as I did. He knew, too, that I was after his job, unless he was a complete fool.

Haines frowned. "You have chosen to go undercover to Gehenna, to pose as the replacement leisure officer. Have you considered a more direct approach?"

"Considered it and rejected it. The advantages of posing as a crew member, in terms of opportunities for true participant observation of the group dynamic, are well-documented. I might quote your own field reports on E. Eridani 3 and on Tau Ceti Orbiter, which are still regarded as classics of a kind..."

I was not being sarcastic. Not entirely, at least. Haines's investigations were classics, and I had learned a great deal from them.

"The technique has its uses, yes. Under the right circumstances. But let me point out that each of those investigations involved a much larger population than our complement on Gehenna. You will be part of a very small work group, and your behavior will come under much more intense scrutiny. The risk of being identified, with all the inevitably counterproductive results, is therefore considerably greater. I don't believe that the potential benefits here are sufficient to justify that risk."

"I have weighed the risks," I said. "I find them acceptable. You see, I will not be identified. I do have some experience with this technique myself, you know."

Haines made no response to this, moving implacably on through some mental checklist.

"Further, by posing as a replacement for the suicided individual, you make yourself the target for the projection of the crew's powerful and unresolved feelings toward their colleague and the manner of his death. This will make your life extremely difficult, and may hinder your ability to investigate."

"I disagree," I said. "I think it will be extremely useful to become a focus for their projections. In fact, I intend to encourage it. I see it as a major advantage."

"My own judgment is that in this case a more honest and open approach would produce the best results."

Haines was being more persistent than I would have expected. Typically he would have given up his nagging by now.

"Deception," I said, "is the shortest path to truth. Or so I have found. Are you instructing me to reconsider my methods?"

There was a pause. Was Haines going to enforce his authority? It would be a striking departure from form.

"Your methods are your own," he said finally. "I will only advise. It is your decision."

It was the usual resolution of our disagreements, although in this case it had taken unusually long to reach.

"I'll let you know," I said. "But I remain inclined toward my original plan."

Haines nodded, as if in acquiescence to the inevitable.

"Take care out there, Lewin," he said. "This situation may be more difficult than you think. I still have a feeling for these things."

He rested his hands lightly on the stack of printed-out reports from Station Gehenna which sat on his desk, as though deriving some clue through the thick plastifold bindings.

And then he muttered something.

"What?" I asked.

"Nous sommes tout sauvages," he said. "Graffiti found in a ruined church, a long time ago and far away. Written when the French were trying to colon-

ize North America, planting down these tiny isolated little outposts in the middle of the wilderness. And finding their civilization unwinding out there, out beyond the social bonds that tie us together, out there in the middle of all that hardship and desolation and savagery. Listening to the forest, feeling its strange power..."

He trailed off, then, apparently embarrassed.

"There are no forests on Gehenna."

"No," he said. "No forests."

8

They were all seated at the mess table when I arrived for third-meal, all of them, the entire station crew, the full population of the planet. All five of them. Previously there had been six, and now once again they were up to a full complement.

Muller rose from his place at the head of the table.

"I believe you've met everyone now," he said, "except Valerie Theron, our science officer and assistant station commander."

Theron, a woman in her late thirties with dark hair and prominent cheek bones, nodded almost imperceptibly, her face as immobile as a mask.

"Welcome aboard," she said—rather oddly, I thought.

This was, of course, the widow of Arthur Duggan.

After Duggan's unfortunate departure, Valerie Theron had been offered a cancellation of her tour of duty by the company, with a full year's salary in recompense.

She had declined, claiming that she was suffering no grief and was perfectly capable of continuing her duties. Her marriage to Duggan, she had explained, had been primarily an arrangement of convenience. Given the company's long-standing preference for bonded

heterosexual units in frontier assignments, they had
paired off to earn the astonishingly high salaries
available in this line of work. Four years out here, with
nothing to spend that money on, and she could de-
vote herself to her personal research interests. And
this, she had informed the company, remained her in-
tention.

The company's strong preference for married couples in these locations, interestingly enough, had been
firmly established by R. G. Spooner himself. Our
founder was a great believer in the value of family life,
even though he had left his wife and children behind
for years at a time to go storming through the galaxy
on his exploration tours.

The company was not unaware that many of its
employees did indeed marry primarily to qualify for
these lush assignments. The marriage of Remus and
McKinley, for example, might well be of a similar order, from McKinley's point of view if not her husband's. Yet few employees would admit as much, and
so cold-bloodedly.

Since the death of her husband, Valerie Theron had
apparently functioned quite reliably. Yet the company would almost certainly have pulled her out, re-
placing her and her late husband with another couple
possessing the necessary combination of skill profiles, but for the circumstances surrounding Duggan's death. Given those circumstances, however, the
company had decided to let things be, at least for the
duration of my investigation. The preference for
bonded couples, after all, was only a preference, not
an invariable and inflexible policy.

Yet in a sense this placed me in an awkward position. The station crew had been led to believe that I was Arthur Duggan's permanent replacement as their leisure officer, booked up for the last two solars of their tour of duty here. I was a stranger, arriving alone and spouseless. One did not have to study Kinsey to anticipate certain problems in the matter of sexual outlets.

Would I, for example, attempt to bond with Theron? If so, would she accept my advances? If not, what bad feeling might pollute the already strained atmosphere of this station? And, if I were rejected by Theron, or if I pursued a different and already contracted-for partner, what havoc might I wreak in the existing pair-bonding situation?

It was a potentially explosive situation. But I would be staying here only three months, not two solars. And though I could hardly try to calm their suspicions by telling them this, I would certainly avoid inflaming them any further. A field investigator, as the manual clearly states, does not and should not engage in sexual relations with the subjects under study. No doubt other investigators might have departed from this rule on occasion in the past, but I had always adhered to it absolutely. It was essential, after all, that I retain my objectivity.

There was, then, a certain tension at the table. As the meal progressed, I saw various glances going back and forth. Theron looking at me to see if I was looking at her. McKinley looking at Theron to see if she was looking at me. McKinley looking at me, Remus looking at McKinley, and so on. This was rather more interesting than the conversation, which was extremely desultory that night. I wondered if they were always this subdued.

"I think we may have a malfunction developing at substation three," Remus told Muller at one point, describing some anomalies in the data flow from there.

"I suppose we should go out there and take a look," Muller said, with no great interest. "Let's see if we can't locate the problem at this end first."

The two came to no conclusion on this question, other than that one or the other of them would think about it.

Later there was a similarly inconclusive exchange between Muller and Theron. The commander reminded the science officer that several progress reports on atmospheric and other planetary changes were overdue. Yet he did not seem overly concerned about the matter, and no new deadline was set in the end.

Sloppy and incomplete procedural work from this unit had been noted at corporate headquarters even before the death of Duggan. The problem, however, had not been judged serious enough to address at that point in time. The company was prepared to tolerate a certain level of inattention to detail. It was not completely atypical of the course of events in such isolated locations, and in itself it did not necessarily signal major problems to come. Yet in this case, clearly, it had.

And so I remained quiet throughout the meal, watching and waiting, giving offense to no one and making my observations. It was a long meal, the crew eating at a snail's pace as if deliberately stretching it out, as if enjoying what passed for conversation at this table. Obviously they did not like being together that much, but they liked still less being apart. It was again not atypical for meal times to assume this sort of disproportionate social and psychological significance.

The time came to remind them of my presence.

"I'm going to be working up a few leisure programs," I announced over dessert. "I was hoping to get your suggestions. I'm open to any input you may have about what you've been doing and what you'd like to see yourself doing in the way of leisure activities. Afterward I'll be asking all of you to work with me on this individually, but I thought now would be as good a time as any to try and set some priorities for the group as a whole."

"You want suggestions?" Remus asked. "I suggest that you leave us alone. Leave us to our own devices."

"That's an interesting point of view," I said, surprised at the vehemence of his reaction. "But the evidence shows that individuals, left to themselves, often do a poor job of planning their leisure."

"What if I don't want you to help me plan my leisure? What if I don't want to plan it at all?"

There was nothing in Remus's profile to predict such strident individualism. On previous missions he had always been a good team player, participating fully in organized leisure activities.

"I can't force anyone to use their free time more creatively," I said. "I can only point out that finding the proper balance between work and play is extremely important to the physical and mental health of the human organism. Vitally so, in conditions of deprivation like this."

"What deprivation?" Remus asked. "We're all having a wonderful time here, aren't we, gang?"

I was surprised that Muller made no move to put Remus in his place.

"At the same time," I continued, "group leisure activities can be extremely valuable in terms of building up social ties between the members and therefore improving the effectiveness of the work group."

"I didn't ask for a lecture," Remus said.

"I'm not trying to give you one. I'm just trying to explain why you would benefit from these programs. As I said, participation is voluntary, although I will be very disappointed should any of you decide in the negative."

"So will I," Muller said, looking around the table and pausing a long moment on Norman Remus. "So will I."

"I know that some of you have your own personal leisure interests," I said. "There's nothing wrong in that. Periods of individualized leisure activity can often be a constructive and appropriate choice, as long as they're balanced out by social activities. In fact, I hope you will look on me as a useful resource person in planning out such personal activity programs. I know you've been through some difficult and unpleasant times here but we must, finally, look after ourselves. We must, as the old Earth saying goes, keep on smiling."

"You look after yourself..." Remus began, but Muller at last moved forcefully to exert his authority.

"Enough," Muller said. "That's enough from you, Norm. Let's listen to what our new leisure officer has to say. He is here, after all, to make our lives easier."

"Vic," I said. "Please call me Vic."

Actually, I despised that or any other contraction of my name. But as a leisure officer, it was necessary for me to encourage conviviality by any means possible.

"Yes," said Vichevski, apparently taking up her husband's cue. "I myself have missed our bridge contests. Haven't you, Norman?"

"Since you ask, no, I don't miss them." His expression was openly hostile now, a hostility out of all proportion to Vichevski's remark. "I don't like bridge. I hate the game. I find it pointless and boring. I was glad when..." He stopped himself, continued more quietly. "I was glad when we stopped playing and gave up our ridiculous charade of being all friends together."

"Tensions," I said, "often develop in small groups like this one, thrown on top of one another in conditions of severe isolation. That's perfectly normal—the company has always recognized that. In fact, that's why the company provides a leisure officer, an otherwise nonfunctional team member, at quite considerable expense."

"Fuck the company," Remus said.

There was a moment of silence.

"Norman..." Muller began.

"You heard me," Remus said. "Fuck the company. The company knows nothing. The company is run by a bunch of fucking idiots. What does the company know? Look at what happened to Duggan. Maybe the company should have provided a leisure officer for the leisure officer."

I stole a glance at Valerie Theron. She seemed unmoved by this reference to her late husband. She sipped her coffee, watching Remus's outburst dispassionately.

"The company is not infallible," Muller said. "The company is not god. No one suggests that it is. The company makes mistakes, and perhaps it made one in assigning Arthur Duggan here..."

"Perhaps it made one in assigning *anyone* here."

"Nevertheless," Muller said, "the correctness of the principle of structured leisure activity has been amply demonstrated. We have two more solars here together. We have to live with one another."

"We don't have to participate in nonsensical activities in our free time. That isn't in my contract, at least. We don't even have to talk to one another off duty, for that matter."

Remus got up and stalked away from the table.

I glanced at Charlotte McKinley. Her expression in viewing these events appeared to be one of mild interest, as though she were watching one of her historic soap operas. She had made no attempt to restrain her husband throughout his outburst, and now made no motion to follow him.

"I must apologize," Muller said, "for this intolerable behavior. I will speak to him privately. I can assure you there will be no repetition of this."

"I should apologize, too," I said. "I should not have rushed into things like that. I should have waited to develop a better feeling for the situation first."

"You will," McKinley told me, "soon enough."

9

I lay in my bed in my unfamiliar quarters, unable to sleep.

Fuck the company, Remus had said. An unexceptional thought, perhaps. Probably almost every employee would have thought it from time to time, seething over some real or imagined injustice—even Muller, even myself. They might even express such a thought aloud, from time to time, to a friend or spouse or trusted colleague. But typically you would not say such a thing in front of your boss, not if you expected to remain employed by this company.

The outburst was all the more surprising in view of what I knew about Remus's background. Remus, of all the people in this station, perhaps owed the most to the company, owed it the unswerving loyalty he had always demonstrated in the past. For Remus, to all intents and purposes, had been raised by the company.

The son of a factory worker in one of the company's original industrial facilities in high Earth orbit, a single mother desperate to escape her permie status, Remus had been educated in the company's schools, lived in its homes, attended its picnics and field trips. And, when his mother had been killed in some squalid after-shift brawl when he was ten, the company had taken on exclusive responsibility for his well-being, housing him in a company-approved foster home and paying for all his expenses, including his later education at Spooner University. Since then, of course, he had worked for the company. He had known no other life.

No question about it, there was a wrongness here. It was most clearly evident in Norman Remus, yet I could feel it in all these people, in the way in which they talked and acted and reacted. And this, of course, was exactly what we had feared.

"One bad apple," Haines had told me, "and the whole barrel goes. Whatever a barrel is or was."

Duggan's death had affected the crew far more than they were prepared to admit. Or else their behavior, like Duggan's death, was the result of some underlying situational dynamic that was still at work here. It was up to me to find out.

In this sense, at least, there was no great novelty in my assignment here. To the mines of Betelgeuse One, to the fisheries of Lakeworld, or to the megafarms of Greenfield, wherever the company sent me, I would go to diagnose the causes of disorder and to prop up sinking morale. For where there was poor morale, there was also the probability of inefficiency. The company had learned that lesson well through long experience in human resources management. And inefficiency, of course, was something it could not afford to tolerate.

In this particular case, of course, more was riding on the outcome than just the effective utilization of

human resources. Although I did not take seriously
Haines's suggestion that the suicide of a minor company official could in itself provoke any great scandal, there was reason for his concern all the same. A
complete collapse of morale here, a failure to cope
with the arduous conditions of this pioneering project, could set an absolutely ruinous precedent.

"Gehenna," I was told in the course of my briefings, "has always been something of a problem spot.
Even at the beginning, when the original construction
crew went in to build the stations. We had a lot of
tension, fights, wildcat strikes. The work finished
three months over deadline and way over budget. It
was a bad situation all around."

It seemed there was something that people found
depressing and upsetting about Gehenna, more so
even than the usual bleak and empty frontier world.
Yet I found that an unsatisfactory explanation of the
difficulties here. Company teams, after all, had operated efficiently in the past in almost equally inhos-
pitable places.

The problem, I thought, had to be with the people.
The balance of the team here was somehow all
wrong—the original readings of compatibility invali-
dated by some unknown error factor. For example, it
could be that the fault lay with Muller's style of leadership here. I had not been much impressed with him
at our first meeting, and I was even less so now after
witnessing his reluctance to bring Norman Remus to
heel at third-meal.

It was true that Muller had functioned well as a station commander in previous postings. Yet a good sta-

tion commander did not lose his leisure officer. A
good station commander did not allow a situation to
run out of control.

With these thoughts still racing through my head, I
gave up any hope of sleep for the moment. I rose from
my bed and dressed to wander aimlessly through the
vast empty corridors of Station Gehenna. Empty, that
is, but for the robot drones wheeling this way and that,
washing and waxing the floor, collecting garbage, and
keeping the station meticulously clean.

I wondered, briefly, if this was really such a good
idea. Possibly these people would develop a greater
sense of social cohesiveness if they were forced to take
on more responsibility for their own collective hy-
giene. I made a mental note to record this notion in my
log. The company, in its all-encompassing benevo-
lence, might be doing too much for its employees.
Look, after all, at how ungratefully and contemp-
tuously my own services as a leisure officer had been
received.

In the outer corridor, beside the door marked Airlock Two, I paused to peer out through an observation portal at the world outside the station.

It was not yet dark out there. This planet, as I recalled, turned on its axis in a cycle of approximately
30 hours, while the station crew attempted to follow
Terran biocycles. But it was not particularly light,
either. Through the thickly shielded window I could
see the storms raging, as if trying to batter down the
station walls.

As I looked at that boiling whiteness, I could not
help but shudder. Gehenna had been well-named,

perhaps too aptly so. One did not expect such whim-
sicality on the part of the company's exploration
teams. No doubt the public affairs department would
come up with something more suitable once the planet
entered the colonization phase.

The turbulence outside, I knew, was created by the
station itself. Even as I walked, the machinery
hummed on, pursuing its relentless program of destroying the very atmosphere out there, of breaking
down and rearranging that whitish murk into a more
desirable mix of oxygen and inert gases.

Roll on the day, I thought.

I strolled on to the door of Airlock Two. On impulse I operated the door control and stepped into the
lock. A row of atmosphere suits stared down at me
from a rack on the wall. I walked across the compart-
ment to the opposite door and placed my hand on the
control.

"Thinking of taking a walk?" said a voice behind
me. "You're forgetting your atmosphere suit."

10

I turned to see Norman Remus standing in the open inner door, a faint smile on his lips. His earlier hostility now seemed to have cooled, or else to be buried beneath an elaborate sarcasm.

"I couldn't sleep," I said. "I was just exploring. Wandering around."

"And you wanted to see where Arthur Duggan made his final exit?"

"He left through this lock?"

"Right," Remus said. "This is where he checked out, so to speak. We found his footprints outside. Bare footprints. In fact, as far as we know, he wasn't wearing any clothes. As if he was on his way to visit a lover."

Remus, for whatever reason, and despite his previous hostility toward me, now seemed almost anxious to talk to me about Duggan's death. Perhaps no one else in the station wanted to.

"Were you surprised? When you heard about it?"

"Oh yes. In more ways than one."

"You couldn't see why he would do it?"

"That's such a boring question. I'm more interested in *how* he did it."

"How?" I repeated. "I don't follow you."

Remus operated the mechanism on the inner door.
It slid into place, shutting us off from the rest of the
station.

I wondered if he wanted to confide some secret. But
he only nodded toward the exit mechanism on the
outer door.

"Open it," he said.

I hesitated.

"Where does this lead? A vehicle bay?"

He shook his head.

"There's only one vehicle bay, and it's attached to
the main lock, on the other side of the station. This
one leads directly out to the surface. Open it."

I stood frozen, my hand on the mechanism. Was
Remus completely out of control? Was he trying to get
us both killed?

"Go on," Remus said. "Try and follow in Duggan's footsteps. Try and repeat history, if you can."

Confused, I took a step backward. Impatiently,
Remus pushed past me. I watched in horror as he operated the door control.

The door did not open.

"Exit denied," said the autovoice of the door, presumably a circuit of the station's mainframe computer. *"Sensors indicate that you are inadequately
protected."*

My heart was still racing, even though it was now
clear that I had been in no real danger. Remus was
grinning from ear to ear.

"Gotcha! You see, you couldn't have gone out
without a suit, even if you had wanted to."

If Remus had simply been trying to frighten me, he had succeeded. Otherwise I didn't see what point he was trying to make.

"Well," I said. "That's good. You made sure that it could never happen again."

"You think we put this safety program in after he died? You're wrong. It was there all along."

"I don't understand," I said, completely baffled now. "Then how did Arthur Duggan go out without a suit?"

"That's an interesting question, isn't it? What do you think?"

I resented being forced to play guessing games with Remus, but clearly he was not going to help me on this unless I made at least a token effort.

"Well, I suppose he must have gone out with a suit on and then taken it off outside."

"Bare feet, remember? In any case, there were no suits missing. In fact, when Duggan went missing we thought at first he must be in the station—because one of the first things we did was count the suits. But he wasn't in the station, we scanned every centimeter of it. Once we started to look out there, we picked him up on the outside monitors, about a half a klick away. But by the time we went out to get him, the winds had blown his body away and we never did find it. There wouldn't have been much worth looking at, anyway."

"Could he have overridden the safety mechanism?"

"Maybe he could have rigged up something, although it wouldn't have been easy. But if you were going to commit suicide, would you bother to do that?

He could have just gone out in a suit and opened his faceplate. Same result, after all.''

I was growing tired of this game.

"Alright," I said. "I can only suppose that the safeguards must have failed. I don't see any other explanation."

"Everything can fail," Remus said. "But the question would then be why they failed at that particular moment."

None of these questions had even been raised in Muller's report on the death of Arthur Duggan. I wondered if Remus was putting me on again. Perhaps there was some simple explanation that he was withholding from me.

"So what's your theory?" I asked. "How did he do it?"

"You figure it out," Remus said. "You're the detective, after all."

"I'm the what?"

"The detective. Isn't that so? They sent you here to find out who killed Duggan."

"Killed Duggan?"

He was moving much too fast for me. There had been absolutely no suggestion of foul play in any of the reports I had read. If there had been, the company would have dispatched one of its security teams rather than a psychological investigative officer.

"Wait a minute," I said. "I understood that this was a straightforward case of suicide. Or maybe, if what you say about the safety mechanisms is true, a little less straightforward. Are you trying to tell me that someone murdered him?"

"I don't think that's a great logical leap. I just explained to you how it couldn't have been suicide. For a detective, you're not very quick on the uptake."

I ignored this new reference to his peculiar fantasy about me.

"If what you say about this safety program is true..."

"It is true."

"If what you say is true, why was this not noted in the original report on Duggan's death?"

"Perhaps you should ask our station commander that."

"I'm asking you."

"Well, obviously Muller overlooked it. The big question is whether he did so deliberately."

"And what does Muller say?"

"He claims it was an oversight, of course. He says it never occurred to him at the time, that he was unaware that the safety mechanism even existed. None of us had ever tried to go outside without a suit, after all."

"Do you think that's true?"

"It could be. Although I would have thought that a station commander of his experience would know everything there is to know about this station."

"But you told him about it in any case. He should still have been able to report it."

"I told him about it as soon as I knew about it. But that was weeks later, after the original report had been filed. At the time, you see, I accepted that it was a suicide. I didn't know about the safety mechanism myself. But there was no reason why I should know—

I'm not the station commander around here. It was only later, when I looked at the matter more closely, that I saw the discrepancy."

"But why did you look into it? What made you suspect there was something wrong here?"

"I had my reasons. The important thing is what I found. And what Muller did, or didn't do, about it."

"Which was?"

"Nothing, really. He looked into it, or claimed to. And he decided to let his original report stand."

"You could have reported it yourself."

"I could have, yes. And you think the company would believe me rather than Muller? It would have ended up with me getting pulled out of here and Muller coming out covered in roses. He's been building quite a file on me, you know, on my so-called performance problems."

"I find it hard to believe that Commander Muller would deliberately suppress important evidence."

"Believe it. Muller has his own reasons for keeping quiet about this."

"Are you trying to tell me that it was Muller? Muller killed Duggan?"

"I didn't say that," he said. "I didn't say who killed him. You'll just have to figure it out for yourself. Like I said, you're the detective."

"But I'm not a detective," I said, in genuine irritation. "You've got it wrong. I'm a leisure officer. Investigating murders is quite outside my job description. That's one of the most ridiculous things I ever heard."

But Remus was quite oblivious to my protests.

"I don't envy you," he said, as he left me standing there in the lock. "I wouldn't want to take on this particular case."

"I'm not a detective," I called after him.

But it was obviously quite hopeless. Paranoid, I thought, the man was paranoid, quite seriously deranged, and I should have discerned as much earlier. This was only further evidence of the seriousness of the situation here.

And yet at the same time, with that peculiar acuteness so often typical of the psychologically marginal, Remus had struck uncomfortably close to the truth of the matter. For I was, in my own way, a detective. And my carefully trained sensitivity to the life of the emotions, along with my intellectual capacity to pick out and synthesize the larger patterns behind the ebb and debris of everyday life, uniquely qualified me to handle this unforeseen development in my investigations at Station Gehenna. For if Arthur Duggan had indeed been murdered, then who better to track down and apprehend his killer? Who better? And should I succeed in this project, how could the company deny me my proper reward?

If I had any firm evidence that Duggan had indeed been murdered, of course, it would be my duty to inform the proper authorities and step aside to allow more qualified personnel to complete this investigation. But as yet there was no more to go on than the wild accusations of an obviously unstable crew member. In reporting them I might only embarrass myself and the company.

For the moment, at least, this investigation remained firmly in the realm of the psychological. If necessary, and at the proper time, I would indeed bow to the superior experience and technology of the security department. At the proper time.

They had never found the body. And as Remus had observed, there wouldn't have been much worth looking at anyway, once Gehenna had done its work. Could Duggan have actually been murdered inside the station, then pushed out the lock? The footprints indicated that he had walked out under his own power, yet perhaps those footprints had been faked somehow. Or perhaps he had still been conscious when his assailant, fully suited, had dragged him outside to die his horrible death. The murderer would then have carefully erased his or her own bootprints.

Yes, I thought, it might easily have happened that way. But if so, then who was the killer?

Perhaps it was Remus himself. The very fact that he now tried to persuade me that Duggan was murdered, while everyone else was content with a verdict of suicide, could be read as evidence of a guilty conscience. Perhaps he could no longer stand to escape unpunished for his crime. Perhaps that was why he saw in me the detective who would bring him to justice.

It was plausible, in a way, if a little too pat. I had never been a great believer in the notion of guilty conscience. And why would Remus want to kill Duggan? Charlotte McKinley, I thought. Perhaps Remus killed Duggan because he was having an affair with his wife, despite the fact that the exogamy clause in his marriage contract gave him no reason to take such offense.

Then again, Remus had implied that Muller had had a hand in this, at least in concealing the fact of Duggan's murder. Could Muller have been the killer? Or could he have been protecting someone else—his wife, perhaps, or another crew member?

With these possibilities whirling around in my head, I fell at last into an exhausted and uneasy sleep.

11

When I arose at last, several hours past first-meal, I thought very carefully about my conversation with Remus the night before. In the cold light of day, it seemed to me that I had allowed myself to become overexcited by Remus's bizarre theories. And yet it was curious all the same that this business of the exit safeguard mechanism had never been reported to corporate headquarters.

If what Remus said was true, then Muller had misled us as to the true facts of the matter. At the least, he was responsible for an error of omission, and it was possible that the matter was a good deal more serious than that.

If Muller had indeed set out to lead us astray, he would have done so with every expectation of success. R. G. Spooner Interplanetary Development Corporation, through both philosophy and necessity, has always been a decentralized operation, delegating great responsibility to the line manager on the spot. In a matter like this one, the company would have trusted his judgement, at least on the technical details. If Muller reported the death of Arthur Duggan as a clear-cut case of suicide, no one would think to question his verdict or to make any more than a cursory examination of the data.

I considered the possibility of approaching Muller, of demanding a fuller explanation of the circumstances surrounding Duggan's death. Yet to do so now would be to demonstrate a possibly excessive concern about these matters. Excessive, at least, for someone claiming to be merely a leisure officer. It might well threaten the security of my carefully fabricated cover identity.

Moreover, if Muller had indeed been involved in a deliberate cover-up as to foul play in the death of Arthur Duggan, he would hardly admit it now. I would succeed only in warning him of my suspicions, and he would become proportionately more vigilant in his defense.

I decided to hold my peace for the moment, and to conduct my own inquiries. As a first step I used the terminal in my room to access the vids of the station crew's testimony in the matter of Arthur Duggan. I had viewed these vids before, of course, back on Earth, without discerning even the faintest suspicion of murder.

"I noticed he was missing in the morning," Valerie Theron had testified, looking a little pale, perhaps, but otherwise quite composed. "I had taken a sleeping medication the night before, so I would not have heard him come in. I thought little of his absence at first. He did not always sleep in our quarters. But I did not see him anywhere in the station all that day, and no one else recalled seeing him either. And so I reported as much to Commander Muller, and we organized a search.

"All atmosphere suits and vehicles were accounted for, and yet Arthur was nowhere in the station. He could only be outside. Outside monitors confirmed as much. We tried to recover his body, although wind and visibility conditions severely hampered our search. We did not find him. His body could have been blown klicks away in the storms.

"Why did he do it? I can offer no special insight. He seemed to change considerably following our arrival here. In the few months I had known him back on Earth he was gregarious, outgoing, more enthusiastic than reflective. Yet here he became increasingly withdrawn and depressed. He did not seem willing to discuss what was bothering him, and I never pressed him to do so. We were never really that close, although of course I regret his death."

"We found the apparent suicide note in the drawer of his desk.... He had never mentioned these dreams to me."

There was more of her testimony, but it was in much the same vein. The interview had been conducted by an autopsy program, an expert system following the long-established protocol in such matters. It did a thorough, clinical job, although there were times when I thought a human interviewer might have pushed harder on one point or another.

"Estimate frequency of sexual contact with the subject," the program asked at one point.

"Initially, two or three times a week," she said. "In the months before his death we had no sexual relations."

I would have followed this matter up. Did she believe that Duggan was entirely celibate in the last few months of his life, or had he been interacting sexually with another member of the station crew? For that matter, had Theron herself been seeking satisfaction elsewhere, and if so how might this have impacted on Duggan's mental state? What had been her attitude to her spouse's withdrawal from sexual contact? Disappointment? Relief? And so on.

In my experience, sexuality, where it is not a positive force, is often a powerfully disruptive factor in the morale of these isolated settlements. Yet the program posed none of these questions, whirring onward to complete its agenda.

"Estimate the subject's alcohol consumption."

"Moderate, as far as I know."

And so on.

The interview did bring home to me just how wildly mismatched Theron and Duggan had been from the beginning: the cool, calm scientist and the warm, outgoing leisure officer. Perhaps he had met some need in her all the same, had temporarily unlocked some previously hidden passion in her make-up. But I did not think it very likely.

Greta Vichevski testified primarily as to the medical aspects of the case.

"Arthur Duggan was ordered by the station commander to attend a medical check-up two weeks prior to his suicide. In his memo to me, station Commander Muller pointed to certain problems in Mr. Duggan's attitude and behavior and asked me to see if there was any medical basis to these problems.

"Mr. Duggan's physical condition appeared reasonably good. However, several problems were observed. His sleep cycle, by his own report, was becoming increasingly desynchronized from the station's schedules. He was going to sleep later each night and rising later each morning. This problem had already been noted by other members of the station's crew and was one of the reasons noted by Commander Muller for referring Mr. Duggan to me.

"Such free cycling is a common problem in offplanet locations, particularly for less-experienced personnel, unused to being detached for long periods of time from the normal Earth referents governing individual biocycles. In itself it is less of a health problem than a work problem, to the extent that it disrupts normal station routines. Arthur Duggan claimed that it did not interfere with his own work, and this was true to the extent that he worked primarily in the evenings. However, regulations on this point are quite clear, and Mr. Duggan promised to make efforts to correct the problem, although he refused medication as an aid to sleep.

"As well as exhibiting sleep cycle problems, Mr. Duggan also appeared depressed. I had noted this before his examination, in everyday interactions, as had other members of the station crew. Commander Muller was concerned that it was affecting Duggan's work. I could find no physiological basis for this condition. I did attempt to draw him into a discussion of what was troubling him, but he insisted that he was feeling fine. As in the case of his sleeping problems, he refused any medication for his condition.

"He never mentioned to me the 'dreams' referred to in his apparent suicide note."

Charlotte McKinley was brief and to the point, yet there seemed something guarded in her expression.

"I last saw him at the evening meal. He ate little. Lately his appetite had seemed poor. He was quiet and withdrawn, as he had been for some time lately. In a way I wasn't surprised when I heard what he had done.

"I always found Arthur Duggan to be a highly conscientious leisure officer, although it is true that he seemed to lose interest a little toward the end.

"I would agree that there was some change in his personality. In some ways, he was no longer the same person at all."

Norman Remus seemed alternately bored and nervous.

"I may have been the last to see him," he said. "In the outer corridor, near Airlock Two, I would guess around 0100. I am often up around that hour—I find that I need less sleep here for some reason. I was on my way back to my quarters. I saw Duggan just standing there, looking outside. I thought little of it, as I often saw him there, at different times of the day. We did not speak—we have never talked much. At first I found him a little too friendly, in a phony sort of way, and later he lost all interest in conversation.

"I left him there and returned to my quarters. I did not see him again."

And finally there was Franz Muller, his bafflement at what had transpired apparently quite genuine.

"Leisure officer Arthur Duggan had been functioning below his expected level of performance for some months. He seemed to show little enthusiasm for his work. He arrived for recreational sessions totally unprepared in a number of instances, and on one or two occasions he failed to show up at all. Moreover, the programs he did prepare seemed to me to be lacking in substance and quality. Documentation on these problems is available if required.

"I had of course confronted him about this several times to little effect. We would sit down together and work out objectives, discuss how the weaknesses in his performance might be corrected. Yet he seemed quite apathetic about the matter, even though I warned him of the possible consequences.

"I did consider requesting a replacement. However, I have had some success before in performance counselling with my subordinates. I was willing to try a little longer. Moreover, if Duggan was recalled at my request, it was probable that his spouse would be recalled too, whatever her own feelings in the matter. I have seen this happen before. I recognize, of course, that the company has good reasons for its procedures, but I have never thought it fair that the performance of one spouse should determine the fate of the other in situations like this. In this particular case, science officer Theron's work had been quite exemplary, and I wished to retain her services here.

"At no point did science officer Theron attempt to influence my decision in this matter. The decision to continue Duggan's employment here was mine alone, and I accept full responsibility for it. And, of course, I deeply regret its consequences.''

He seemed unusually insistent on this point. Could he, in fact, have yielded to pressure from Theron to keep on Arthur Duggan? What influence might Theron have upon him? If she did have such influence, might it extend even to protecting her from the consequences of murdering her husband?

"Initially, I thought of Arthur Duggan as a very gregarious sort of fellow, although perhaps this was some sort of pose. In any case, he appeared to go through a great transformation. I have no definite explanation for this. If you ask me to speculate, I might suggest that he was experiencing marital difficulties, but this is pure supposition. It may be that he was not really cut out for this kind of work. He had never worked before in such a highly isolated location.''

How would Muller know of Theron's marital difficulties? Perhaps she had confided them to him. Or perhaps, I thought, he himself was the cause of them.

12

Following my review of these vids, it was necessary for me to put my investigations to one side for the moment to concentrate on working up a group recreation program.

That evening, I made my official debut as leisure officer. In all honesty, I must concede that it was not a conspicuous success. The attendance, for one thing, was less than impressive. Norman Remus, perhaps not unexpectedly, failed to show up at all. Valerie Theron arrived only to excuse herself, pleading lower back pain from too long a session at her laboratory workbench.

"Enough for bridge," Greta Vichevski had said brightly, and I feared for a moment that her suggestion would carry the day. My own views on the game were quite close to those of Remus.

As it turned out, McKinley was not keen, and I was able to introduce my crewmates to the joys of *Galactic Empire*, a new interactive vid/board game lately the rage back on Earth. My trainer in leisure leadership back on Earth had assured me that it was engaging without being terribly demanding, a good ice-breaker for any program.

"I see," said Vichevski, after I had stumbled through the rules. "The idea is to build up your own empire. It sounds intriguing. But where do the corporations come in?"

"There are no corporations in this game," I said. "You're a galactic emperor, out to conquer new star systems. Corporations don't come into this at all."

"It's a fantasy game," McKinley pointed out.

"What a pity," Vichevski said. "I'm sure Franz would enjoy it much better if he could be a corporation. Not just any corporation, of course. It would have to be Spooner Interplanetary. Franz wouldn't want to be one of our competitors."

"Of course not," Muller said. "I am nothing if not a good company man."

Although Muller seemed to take no offense at his wife's comment, I was, to say the least, surprised by it. Even though disguised as humor, the implied criticism seemed quite clear. She was being, I thought, indiscreet at the very least, and perhaps even actively hostile. Whether or not Muller was a good company man, it was not the sort of thing you expected to hear from a good company wife.

"Perhaps Franz could be the Emperor Spooner," McKinley suggested.

Muller took this joshing, too, in good part.

"I'll enjoy this well enough," he said mildly.

I wondered whether, given the choice, he would willingly choose to participate as an equal with his subordinates in these recreational activities. But the company left him no such choice. For Muller, at least, participation in these programs was mandatory—a

necessary counterbalance to his otherwise almost un-
trammelled authority over his people.

In this sense, at least, I held a certain power over
him. However foolish he might think the programs I
proposed, he would have to join in them all the same.
No doubt this would have been a cause of additional
friction between him and Duggan if Duggan's own
programming efforts had really been as poor as they
appeared. Although in itself this would hardly be a
motive for murder.

And so Muller participated, but he would not necessarily enjoy it. He would not enjoy his wife's taunt-
ing him about his possibly excessive dedication to the
company in front of his subordinates. He would not
enjoy being teased by the nutrition officer.

We played *Galactic Empire* for several hours, although I do not think any of us enjoyed it very
much—not even McKinley, who showed a sound
strategic sense and quickly built up an almost impreg-
nable lead.

I could blame this lack of enjoyment on the game,
which was indeed rather a silly one, but the fault was
in large part my own. I was simply unable to perform
my role in terms of generating the appropriate social
dynamics. Nor did it help when my understanding of
the rules proved somewhat shaky, leading to
considerable and repeated confusion.

At the conclusion Muller rose and thanked me pro-
foundly.

"It has been most diverting and entertaining," he
said, "and I anticipate many more such happy eve-

nings together. Unfortunately, I must now take my leave and attend to certain procedural matters.''

"So conscientious,'' said Vichevski, as her husband left the room.

She stood up, too.

"And now I believe I will go and scan a book,'' she said.

McKinley made no motion to leave. We stared at each other across the table.

"I was disappointed that Norman couldn't be with us tonight.''

"Norm doesn't like games. He doesn't like much of anything.''

"I ran into him last night, quite late,'' I said. "I couldn't sleep so I was wandering around.''

"We all have problems getting to sleep from time to time. Norm has it worse than me.''

"What about Arthur Duggan?'' I asked. "Did he have problems sleeping, too?''

"I suppose he did,'' she said. "You seem very interested in Arthur. That's the second time you've asked me about him.''

"I'm curious. I feel a certain kinship for him. I am, after all, his replacement.''

"Yet you're nothing like him.''

"Did Norm mention that we had talked?''

"No, he didn't. What did you talk about?''

"About Arthur Duggan, actually. Although he raised the subject, not me.''

"What about Arthur?''

"About how he died.''

"He's dead," she said flatly. "What difference does it make how he died?"

"No difference, I suppose. I'm sorry if I've upset you...."

"You didn't upset me. But I've already heard this too often from Norm. He told you that it was murder, right? That someone pushed him out, or took him out in a suit and brought the suit back empty? Something like that?"

"He didn't really suggest how it was done. He just implied that there was something more to Duggan's death than a simple suicide."

"I wouldn't take Norm's theories too seriously if I were you. I don't think he takes them seriously himself."

"But the exit safeguard..."

"Ah yes, of course, the famous exit safeguard. What about it? It didn't work, that's all. Lots of things around here don't work. There was a glitch, no more. As I've told Norm a dozen times."

"A very convenient glitch."

"I don't have any problem with it myself. But if it wasn't a glitch, then Arthur must have figured out some way to fool the safety program. It wouldn't have been that hard. He could have written a little program to communicate with the door circuit and tell it everything was OK."

"If he knew how to program."

"He knew how. He worked a lot with computers. He used to write his own games."

"But would someone who wanted to commit suicide go to so much trouble?" I asked, echoing Remus's question.

"I suppose he might, if he was determined to commit suicide in a particular way. But I think we're complicating matters unnecessarily. It was just a glitch. Norm is seeing problems where none exist, and now he's got you seeing them, too."

"Yet none of this was mentioned in the original autopsy report. And that report was never amended."

"You've scanned the autopsy report? Norm must have really got you going."

"But he may have a point. I don't understand why no one mentioned this, either at the time or later."

"No one thought of it at the time. *I* didn't think of it, certainly, until Norm started going on about it. And even Norm didn't think about it until weeks after it happened. When someone kills himself, you don't go around thinking about exit mechanisms. I didn't even know that safety program existed."

"Muller should have known."

"So Norm says, and perhaps he should have. Perhaps he did know, but didn't think about it. He's only human, after all—he can't be expected to remember everything. Norm only found out about it when he pulled the specs on the door circuit from the file."

"Why did he pull the specs?"

"Because he likes to make simple things complicated."

"So he told Muller about it . . ."

"Yes. Almost immediately after he found out about it. Even though I told him he was going to make a fool of himself."

"And Muller did nothing about it?"

She looked surprised.

"But he did! He thanked Norm for his information. He checked the safety program, which seemed to be working normally. And then he pulled apart the door circuits. And he found a number of components which were worn or faulty to varying degrees and which may well have been subject to intermittent failure. Norm knows all this. He saw the components himself. He didn't tell you about it?"

I shook my head.

"He just told me that Muller decided to let his original report stand."

"Well, there you are, you see. Norm is trying to involve you in this conspiracy theory of his by leaving out the important facts."

"Still, it isn't conclusive. What Muller found."

"No, but it's suggestive. And surely it makes more sense to suppose that there was a glitch than to suppose that someone killed Arthur. Who would want to kill him, after all?"

"Yet Muller never modified his original report."

"No. He saw no reason to. It wouldn't make him look good, the fact that he had overlooked that safety program in the first place, and pointing it out now would achieve no purpose. It was still suicide, after all."

No doubt she was right. The company didn't like suicide very much, but it would be even less enthusiastic about murder. Given the new facts, it would have gone for the glitch theory every time. And that could well be the correct theory.

It was true that Muller was at least technically in default here, in the sense that he should have left that decision up to headquarters rather than take it on himself. But McKinley's arguments were persuasive. It seemed likely to me now that there was nothing more sinister here than a suicide, which Remus, for some paranoid reason of his own, had chosen to overcomplicate.

Investigating that suicide would be demanding enough without giving myself additional and wholly irrelevant problems solving a nonexistent mystery. But I felt disappointed all the same.

"I suppose you're right," I said.

"Don't take my word for it," she said. "Ask Muller, ask Theron, ask anyone but Norm. It was suicide, for sure."

"You don't seem to have a high opinion of your husband's opinion."

"My husband is a little . . . disturbed. As I'm sure you must by now have figured out for yourself."

"Disturbed by what?" I asked. "By Duggan's death?"

"Before," she said. "It's got worse since then, but it started well before that, quite early in the tour. And yet it had to do with Duggan all the same."

"How?"

"Norm became obsessed with the idea that Arthur and I were involved, sexually speaking. He became quite jealous and possessive, even though he had no reason to do so—our contract quite clearly permits exogamy."

"And were you?"

"Were we what?"

"Involved?"

"Sexually? I don't really see how that concerns you, Mr. Lewin."

"Call me Vic. I'm sorry—you're right. It doesn't. But let me ask you this. Do you think Norm might have killed Duggan?"

There was a pause.

"You do ask a great many questions," she said. "I'm starting to wonder whether Norm might not be right for once."

"About what?"

"About you," she said. "He thinks you're a detective. Come here to investigate Arthur's death, to make sure that there was no—what do they say?—*foul play* involved. Crazy though that sounds, perhaps you are."

I laughed uneasily.

"I can assure you that I am not a detective."

"In a way, I wish you were. It would be quite exciting. And we could certainly use some excitement around here. Not to criticize your recreational programs, of course."

"Perhaps I should break out the *Clue*."

"Clue?"

"Classic old Earth detective game. We should have one in stock here. But seriously, suppose I was a detective, and suppose Arthur was murdered, whom should I suspect?"

"There you go again," she said. "I already told you
it was suicide—there's no reason to think anything
else."

"I'm playing detective now," I said. "It's more fun
than *Galactic Empire*. Who would be the number one
suspect?"

"Norman, I suppose. If he wasn't the one trying so
hard to persuade everyone that there was a murder."

"Say it was Norman all the same. What would be
his motive?"

"Jealousy. A crime of passion."

Despite herself, I could see that she was warming to
the game.

"Sounds logical."

"Of course, there could be another motive. Money,
for example. Perhaps Norman is a saboteur, bribed by
a rival corporation to destabilize the station and wreck
the company's development plans."

"Good," I said, excited. "Or the motive could be
ideological. He could be a political subversive, some
sort of militant Contractionist."

She laughed aloud at that idea.

"Norm a Contractionist? That's hard to believe. I'll
stick with jealousy. It's more flattering, in any case."

"Actually," I said, "if sabotage was the motive, we
could hardly exclude anyone here as a suspect. Not
even you."

"How exciting," she said. "But perhaps we're getting a little carried away here. After all, if there was a
saboteur here, why would he want to kill Arthur? If I
wanted to sabotage this place, I doubt that I would

begin with the leisure officer, who is not exactly, with all due respect, a key individual in this set-up.''

"No more than the nutrition officer.''

"People do have to eat," she said, "although I suppose they could program for themselves.''

"Still," I said, "you may have a point. If I were a saboteur perhaps I would kill Muller or Theron or even Norm before I killed anyone else. Yet Duggan for some reason may have represented an easier target. Or he may have somehow stumbled across the saboteur's activities, and therefore had to be eliminated.''

"How very exciting," she said. "This really is a lot more fun than *Galactic Empire*. What a pity that Arthur committed suicide after all, leaving no crime for us to investigate.''

"Yes," I agreed. "What a pity.''

13

Whether or not there was something suspicious in the death of Arthur Duggan, and at this point I was inclined to doubt it, I had a job to do in terms of observing the operations of this station and investigating the morale of its crew.

It was quickly apparent that, from a sociotechnical standpoint, Station Gehenna was a textbook case in bad design. It was a poorly designed environment for working and an even less desirable one for living, but perhaps the most fundamental problem was that of job design. In the days that followed, as I observed the routines of the station's crew, I realized just how little work of any sort they were required to do here—and how harmfully this absence of meaningful work was impacting upon their morale.

Station Gehenna was an almost entirely automated system. The human members of its crew served primarily as standby personnel. They had few regular duties, and even many of these were transparently make-work tasks.

As station commander and chief techperson, Franz Muller had probably the heaviest workload. He attended to the general administration of the station. He also shared responsibility for monitoring various maintenance schedules with Remus. But the administrative work in running this small station was comparatively light, and the maintenance work itself was carried out largely by automated subsystems. Certainly Remus seemed to have a good deal of free time on his hands in which to develop his morbid fantasies of crime and punishment.

Theron gave every appearance of being busy. She would disappear into her workroom for days at a time, sometimes not even emerging for third-meal. Yet her duties in regard to the station, as outlined in her job description, were far from onerous, and even then she seemed somewhat neglectful of them. Presumably she was devoting herself to personal research in there; that or else screening antique soapies.

McKinley and Vichevski, like myself, were purely support personnel. McKinley at least had meal programming to occupy her some part of the day. Vichevski's role was even more limited. Sickness, at least of the sort she could cure, was rare in the isolated world of the station. Yet Space Administration regulations decreed that every permanent installation, no matter how small its personnel complement, should have a medical officer available at all times. And so Vichevski sat in her surgery, scanning medical journals and keeping her surgical skills sharp by operating various simulation programs.

The whole station might as well have been run by one person, like the lighthouses of old Earth. Yet experience had proved that this one person, alone in the face of infinity, would face a small yet significant possibility of going mad. Two was little better, with the probability of violence escalating even as the risks of insanity diminished, and three was even worse. Indeed, long experience in studying the social dynamics of frontier work groups had indicated that you needed not less than six individuals to establish a relatively stable situation, all other things being equal. But of course, all other things were not always equal.

Rather than working together as a smoothly running team, the crew of Station Gehenna had gone through some process of social atomization, flying off in all directions in pursuit of their own interests and obsessions.

To some degree this could only be the fault of Franz Muller. Clearly he had failed to exercise the qualities of leadership necessary to maintain discipline and social cohesion here. And to some degree, perhaps, it could be blamed on the unfortunate Arthur Duggan for failing to provide the structured leisure activities which would have helped glue these individuals together as a true community. Yet I was beginning to wonder whether the real responsibility for their difficulties lay elsewhere.

It was almost as if this team had been handpicked for failure. Norman Remus, for example, was visibly unstable, and I feared that his behavior could only continue to deteriorate. Surely there would have been some warning of this in his previous work record, or in his most recent psychological profile? And had no consideration been given to the potential for serious problems in his marriage to Charlotte McKinley, problems which might undermine his work performance here?

And as for Arthur Duggan, he had never been stationed further from Earth than Mars, and then in an installation with more than one thousand fellow workers. Had no one foreseen his failure to cope with these more arduous circumstances?

Even Muller, whatever his past record, seemed obviously lacking in the qualities of leadership necessary to maintain control here.

Given the high priority placed by the company on the success of this terraforming project, and given the vast capital expenditures committed to this far-reaching plan, this failure on the selection side of things seemed all the more curious. I recalled my joking conversation with McKinley about saboteurs. In fact, I thought, someone could have sabotaged this project just as efficiently without ever leaving Earth.

Could one of the company's great rivals, such as WirtzRaum or Tahiki Development, somehow have placed a mole within the upper reaches of our human resources department? Could Contractionists be at work here? Or could it be someone within the company, one of those within the senior management who had initially opposed this gargantuan project and now wished to see it fail?

It was then I recalled that the executive vice president for human resources was none other than Ronald C. Spooner, Ron Jr., the son and apparent heir of the great R. G. Spooner himself. He would have had the final word on personnel selection for this station. Could Ron Jr. have deliberately sabotaged his own company, his own father's pet project? It was not a thought I wished to consider too closely.

14

Since our conversation on my first night in the station, Norman Remus had been avoiding me. He continued to boycott our increasingly desultory recreational sessions and remained silent through our meals together, apparently preoccupied with his own thoughts.

I was content to let matters stand this way for the moment. Ultimately I would indeed have to consider the question of Norman Remus, and make some recommendations as to his future career. But I saw little to be gained by engaging in further conversation with him and becoming further enmeshed in his delusions about Duggan's supposed murder.

In the second week following my arrival, Remus presented me with even more compelling evidence of his growing eccentricity. Having concluded my recreational activities for the night, I was following the curve of the outer corridor on my way back to my quarters when I saw a figure in the distance, staring through the observation portal beside Airlock Two.

As I drew closer I saw that it was Norman Remus. He did not appear to notice my approach but continued to stare out, as if entranced.

I followed his gaze. It was a compelling sight. The very atmosphere seemed alive, battering away at our station as if determined to crack it open like some fragile eggshell and spill us out upon the face of the planet. Just thinking about it left a feeling of tightness in my stomach.

It was hard to imagine venturing out there, even fully suited and within the safety of a vehicle. Arthur Duggan had chosen a highly effective form of suicide.

Assuming that Remus would have no wish to speak to me, and quite happy to go along with that decision, I nodded to him and was about to walk on by when he turned around and fixed me with his nervous, darting eyes.

"How's it going?" he asked, contriving a casual manner.

"The leisure program? It's going great guns. You missed a most exciting simulated ski tournament tonight."

"Your investigation," Remus said. "How is your investigation going?"

"I'm not investigating anything," I said.

His expression showed disbelief.

"Although," I said, "purely as a matter of curiosity, I did look into the questions you raised about Duggan's death and I'm satisfied . . ."

"You talked to Muller?"

"No," I said. "I just asked around and . . ."

"Charlotte, then," he said, becoming angry now. "You talked to Charlotte and she told you that I'm nuts, right?"

"No," I said. "I did talk to her but she didn't . . ."

"You can believe what you like. But whatever is going on here, Charlotte is part of it."

Remus's conspiracy theory seemed to widen its bounds day by day.

"You're accusing Charlotte now? Your own wife?"

"I'm paranoid, right? Tell me something I don't know."

Abruptly, his anger seemed to burn out. He shook his head, almost sadly. And then he said, "I'm not sure she is my wife. She's not the same person at all."

I wasn't sure how to respond to this statement.

"People change," I said neutrally.

"Yeah. Like Arthur Duggan."

He seemed to lose interest in the conversation. He turned back to the portal.

"I suppose it doesn't really matter what you think."

Once again he stared outside with intense concentration.

"What are you looking for?" I asked. "Out there?"

"Go away," Remus said over his shoulder. "Go investigate somebody else."

I hesitated. I did not much wish to continue this conversation, and yet it was possible I could learn something from it.

"Duggan used to do the same thing," I observed. "Look out there."

Remus continued his vigil.

"Why was that, do you think?" I asked. "Was he thinking about taking a walk out there, nerving himself up to it . . ."

"You think I want to do the same thing?" Remus asked, turning back toward me at last. "Is that what you think?"

"Do you?"

"No. No way. Absolutely not."

"Then what's the attraction?"

"You don't feel it, do you?"

"Feel what?"

"Feel whatever it is that's out there."

He made his somewhat startling statement in an entirely conversational manner, as if we were discussing the menu for third-meal.

"Out there?" I echoed. "You mean the storms?"

Remus gestured impatiently.

"Of course I don't mean the storms. I mean something alive. Out there, waiting for us. Hating us, loving us, whatever."

Despite Remus's previous erratic behavior, and despite my confident expectation of a continued deterioration in his condition, I was still taken aback by this statement. It moved his delusions to an entirely new plane of reference. The man was decompensating before my very eyes.

For all my animistic fantasies of the vengeful storms, I knew very well that nothing lived out there on the bleak surface of Gehenna. Nothing, that is, beyond very limited forms of plant life of the most rudimentary and uninteresting nature. This had been well established by rigorous and scrupulous survey procedures.

I wondered if Remus was trying to play some new game with me. Yet he seemed perfectly serious.

"That's crazy," I said. "There's nothing out there, nothing to speak of, at least. The survey..."

"The survey lied," he said matter-of-factly. "The company lied—it often does, you know, when it's convenient to do so. There's something out there, watching, waiting. I feel it—I think everyone does, although you won't hear them admit it. I know Duggan felt it."

"He told you that?"

"Not in so many words. But I would see him standing here, just watching. Sometimes I would think he even heard it, heard it speaking to him. He would get this blank look in his eyes and stand very still as if he was listening."

"Tell me," I said, carefully. "Do you hear it, too?"

"No. I never have. Not yet."

He looked at me closely.

"You don't believe me," he said. "That's alright. You don't know the score around here yet. But you will."

He turned away from me and pressed his face against the glass of the portal. His whole body shivered.

"You think this was connected with...with what happened to Duggan?"

"I don't know. Maybe Duggan wanted to report this to the Space Administration, wanted to get the terraforming program stopped. Because if there is something out there, then for sure we're killing it. So maybe the company stopped him before he could stop the company. I don't know. You figure it out. You're..."

"I know," I said. "I'm the detective."

Something, I thought as I walked back to my quarters, would have to be done about Norman Remus. And soon. I might not have the luxury of taking the full three months to complete my report here. If Muller failed to assess the situation accurately and take the appropriate action, I might have to identify myself to him in order to warn him of the problem.

The company, after all, would hardly appreciate a second suicide here. Nor would it reflect particularly well on me.

15

Again, that night, it took me a long time to fall asleep. And when at last I slept it was restlessly, disturbed by strange and vivid dreams. Dreams of the world outside the station, dreams of the storms. It was as if I stood naked on the surface of this planet and breathed its ineffably sweet air.

There were no storms: all was tranquil, as it must have been here before the company built its stations. I walked through soft white mists upon soft beds of brilliant white moss, over gently rolling hills. And as I walked I heard ... voices. Soft, crooning, ecstatic, erotic voices, calling to me.

And then the storms came up, battering away at me. And my lungs choked on the new harshness of the air. And the moss began to wither and shrivel at my feet. And still I heard voices, carried on the winds. But now they spoke to me of rage and pain as well as love.

I ran in fear from these voices, and yet they followed me, continued to make their demands on me. And now I was completely lost. I would never find the station again, but would wander forever across this blasted wilderness....

Reviewing these dreams the next morning, I had no difficulty in accounting for them adequately. They represented information processing activity of a very low order. My conversation with Remus, and my own slight apprehensions about the world outside the station, had been played back to me in almost raw form, with certain infantile overlays of sexuality and agoraphobic anxiety.

Yet for all my logical analysis, these dreams lingered in my mind, disturbing me at some deep level. I decided, then, that I must at the earliest opportunity venture outside the safe and secure world of the station and confront the world outside—confront it directly and in the process utterly demystify it, once and for all.

I had already wasted enough time and energy on Norman Remus's delusion of some plot to dispose of Arthur Duggan. I would not allow him to entrap me in his madness again.

"I would like to go outside," I told Muller over first-meal.

"Really?" He seemed surprised. "That isn't part of your duties, you know. And it isn't terribly pleasant out there, I can tell you. Why would you want to do that?"

"Just to look around," I said. "To see and understand this planet, so I can better adapt to the situation in which I find myself. I believe that where there is understanding there can be no mystery and therefore no reason for fear. Not, of course, that I am afraid."

"On the contrary," said Greta Vichevski. "Where there is understanding there can only be mystery, and perhaps also a healthy tinge of fear. Because we can never understand everything, and this is something we also come to understand."

"There may be something in what you say," I said, startled and a little puzzled by this manifestation of a previously unsuspected philosophical streak in our medical officer, but unwilling to be drawn into some lengthy sophomoric debate. "Still, I would like to go outside."

"You know that no one may go outside alone," Muller said. "Station regulations do not permit it, except under certain clearly defined emergency conditions."

It had not, in fact, occurred to me to go outside alone.

"Perhaps I could accompany another crew member on some routine mission."

"It can be arranged. Although you will have to wait until one of us needs to go outside in the course of our duties. This will happen soon enough, but in the meantime no one is going to go out there without some good reason."

"Except Duggan," Remus said, giving me a knowing sort of look. "And possibly he, too, had a good reason."

Muller glared at Remus. But Remus seemed impervious to his commander's anger.

"Perhaps," Remus continued, "this is some inherent personality flaw among leisure officers. A desire to hurl themselves, lemming-like, into the great outside."

Muller raised his hand, palm outstretched.

"Enough," he said. "I will accept no more of your nonsense, Norman. I can, and will, replace you if need be. And we will have no more discussion of Duggan. We will close that chapter of our lives. If nothing else, think of science officer Theron's feelings."

Valerie Theron, who had sat quietly through this exchange, now spoke up. If Muller had believed he was protecting her, Theron's response was intended to demonstrate that she required no such protection.

"I believe, Norm," she said, "that you are unnecessarily maligning the poor little lemming. Contrary to popular misconceptions, lemmings do not in fact engage in periodic bouts of mass suicide—do not deliberately hurl themselves over cliff tops and into great hurtling rivers. Leisure officers, of course, are another question again, and there is little documented evidence as to their propensities."

There was a moment of silence.

"Are you sure about the lemmings?" McKinley asked finally. "I could have sworn I saw a vid . . ."

"A product of clever editing, no doubt," Theron said. "Or perhaps they merely took a few buckets of lemmings and threw them off the cliff. Where reality does not conform to our preconceptions, we have ways of pushing it into shape."

She took a final bite of her toast, wiped her hands carefully on her napkin, and rose from the table.

"If you'll excuse me," she said. "I have work to do."

A further silence followed her departure. She was, I reflected, a creature of almost pure intellect. Or at least, such was the impression she liked to project to the world. In theory, at least, I found this an admirable quality, one I might aspire to myself. Having seen it in practice, I found it not a little chilling.

"Science officer Theron," Muller said, "has been under some strain. The shock of Duggan's death has affected her more than she cares to admit."

"Of course," I said. "Of course."

"All the more reason," Muller said, staring directly at Remus, "why there must be no further talk of Duggan. No more. On this point I must and will insist."

16

I could not say that I looked forward keenly to my trip
into the great outside. Yet it was something, I thought,
that had to be done. I felt this more keenly with each
passing day, as the dreams continued to disturb my
sleep.

The truth was that I had never cared much for nature, even in its mildest forms.

In the early years of our marriage, Rosemary and I
had on occasion taken camping trips, piling our gear
into a rented jeep and heading for the hills. We went
not to the commercial camping areas, where the
permies parked their brightly painted campers under
the stars to plug their vidscreens into the electric
sockets on the trees and close their flowery curtains
against the modest terrors of the stunted woods, but
to the true wilderness parks. Some few of these parks
remained. With industry increasingly heading off into
space, the impulse to ravage them had waned.

It was Rosemary, not I, who affected a great love of
the outdoors. Perhaps it was a genuine love, although
it was also then a fashionable one. All our friends, it
seemed, were taking off to commune with nature, and
Rosemary was nothing if not fashionable.

Personally I was usually miserable on these trips and made little effort to conceal it. It was always too hot for me, or else too cold; the black flies were insufferable, or else the mosquitoes; the ground was too lumpy for a good night's sleep, and the wildlife too noisy. Rapids awaited at every turn in the river, my hands blistered from paddling the canoe, my feet ached from trudging the portage trails.

I remember one occasion when I sat shivering inside a tent, wrapped in a blanket, listening to the rain pouring down for the second day in succession, and wondering when it would begin to drip through the saturated fabric, thinking about the warmth and dryness of the jeep parked outside.

"There was a motel about a hundred kilometers back," I observed. "If we start now, we could probably get there in time for the late vid."

Rosemary looked up from her book.

"This is nothing," she said. "Nothing at all. Last month Ben and Jill hiked thirty kilometers a day for a week, and it rained like this every day."

As if in reply, I sneezed vigorously.

"This is fun," Rosemary told me. "Sitting in here, listening to the rain, breathing the air."

I've had more fun cleaning rat cages, I wanted to say. *I've had more fun getting bitten by the rats.* But I said nothing.

"Don't look at me like that," Rosemary said. "It's just pathetic. You're so controlled, Victor. You're just incapable of opening yourself up to experience."

"That's not true," I said. "I'm just not very interested in nature. Especially not when I'm coming down with pneumonia."

I blew my nose.

"Controlled and controlling," she said. "You just can't stand for anyone else to have any fun. You can't let yourself go, and you're afraid to let anyone else be free."

Rosemary had always had a good line in psychobabble, although in the first flush of romance I had accepted such statements as keenly insightful. Only later did I realize that she had only a small stock of these observations, which she permutated endlessly. She had acquired them, I learned, while still a graduate student and blocked on her thesis, at a weekendlong psychobabble marathon out near the heliport. Following that weekend, pearls of wisdom on ancient and modern soap opera had fallen upon her from the skies.

Her particular brand of psychobabble was known as PsychoAutonomy Training, a prepackaged course offered by deeply tanned, former real estate salespersons, which purported to assist us in confronting both our freedom and unfreedom in this increasingly complex world. Rosemary always referred to it as just "The Training," as in "Victor, you really ought to take The Training."

"Ah, well," I said mildly. "Perhaps you should take these trips with Ben and Jill."

"Perhaps I will," she said. "You know, Ben invited me to come hang-gliding with him during the

Easter vacation. He has a friend who runs a school out in Denver."

"Oh, really," I said. "And Jill?"

"Jill has to stay here and finish her thesis. Anyway, she doesn't like heights."

"I see," I said.

I wondered if she was just punishing me for spoiling her camping trip, or if she was serious around going to Denver with Ben. At this point in our marriage we had not yet resolved our issues about monogamy. Or rather, as Rosemary always pointed out, I had not resolved *my* issues.

"You're so controlling, Victor," she said again. "I think that's what you can't stand about the wilderness. It offends you because you can't control it. You feel that it's controlling you. You can't stand anyone or anything placing limits on your precious personal freedom. You just can't give up control, can't let yourself go for a moment."

"I came camping with you, didn't I?" I asked. "I let you persuade me to come to this godforsaken place."

"But you resent every moment of it," she said. "You've really got to learn how to deal with your attitudes toward freedom and control. You've really…"

"I know," I said. "I know. I've really got to take The Training."

17

"You're in luck," Muller told me one morning at first-meal, at the start of my third week at Station Gehenna.

"I am?" I asked, still drowsy from another unsatisfactory night's sleep, not following his meaning at all.

"You wished to go outside the station," he reminded me. "Well, science officer Theron is going out in a groundcar today to pick up some samples. Usually Norm or myself would go with her, but since you expressed an interest I am assigning you to accompany her."

Now that I had my wish, I regretted ever having wished it. The idea of leaving the comfortable confines of the station to wander through the murk outside was in no way appealing. But the dreams had continued to haunt my sleep. And in any event, I could hardly back down now.

I looked at Theron, who was sitting across from me at the mess table, methodically working through a plate of scrambled synthed eggs. She returned my stare coolly. She did not seem enthusiastic about the idea either.

"When do we start?" I asked her.

"Right now," she said, putting down her fork and getting up from the table.

I gulped down coffee and followed her to Airlock One, where Remus assisted us in climbing into our suits.

"Lovely weather for a drive," he told me, as I walked into the tunnel leading to the vehicle bay.

A few minutes later we were in the groundcar, jolting through the vehicle door of the station and out onto the bumpy surface. The winds outside were fierce, seeming to threaten to blow us right back into the station despite the powerful engine driving the groundcar's treads. But as we left the station behind, the turbulence eased noticeably.

Watching the great and comforting bulk of the station recede behind us and finally disappear into the murk, I felt a flicker of panic. It was scary to be out there, even while doubly protected by suit and groundcar.

"How long," I asked Theron, "could someone survive out there? Without a suit?"

"How long could you hold your breath? Actually, perhaps not even that long. It's possible that the heat would kill you first."

She tapped the outside temperature gauge on the dash. The reading was over 90° Centigrade.

"Before we came here, it used to be a lot hotter than that," she told me. "The dust has cooled things down tremendously."

"Dust?"

I recalled, now, the darkish patches mottling the face of Gehenna that I had seen from space.

"Before they built the stations they set off a series of nuclear explosions, designed to blanket the planet with dust. To create a nuclear winter, in other words, and bring down surface temperatures. That was part one of the terraforming program."

"They used nukes here? I didn't know that was allowed."

"Clean ones. Minimal radioactive fallout. And, of course, they waited for the radiation to come down to acceptable levels before they came in to build the stations."

This aspect of the development program for Gehenna was news to me. Public affairs had obviously played it down to the vanishing point.

"And the Space Administration gave permission?"

"When did the SA ever refuse a development company permission to do anything? I don't recall ever hearing of that happening. But in any case there was no reason for them to refuse. It was a very carefully planned operation."

The cooling down of Gehenna, which still continued, had greatly facilitated the terraforming process.

"We've made a big difference on this planet already," she told me.

After just a few solars of operating the stations, she explained, oxygen readings were up already, over two percent and climbing fast.

"We're concentrating on breaking down the carbon dioxide. Once we get the oxygen up it will take care of the methane and the ammonia."

Earth, she told me, had probably been much like this once, until the algae in the oceans got to work on the carbon dioxide.

"Why didn't we just bring some algae here?"

"There was no permanent ground water down here on the surface," she said. "It was just too hot. We're only starting to get some now. So there was no place to put our algae, anyway, unless we were going to seed the upper atmosphere. But whichever way we went, it would have been a very slow solution. It would have taken hundreds of years, maybe thousands. Obviously the company wanted quicker results than that. And we're getting them."

I paid careful attention to what the company had wrought as we jolted onward, the car following a pre-programmed course toward a beacon planted by Theron on an earlier expedition.

If this was progress, this bleak landscape I saw from the window of the car, it was hard to imagine what this planet had looked like before.

"Overwhelming and merciless," I muttered to myself.

"What?"

"Out there," I said, gesturing. "A phrase that happened to pop into my mind. 'Overwhelming and merciless forces of destruction.' Sigmund Freud on the external environment we all must confront. And he, of course, was talking about Earth. Or even more specifically, I suppose, Vienna."

"Perhaps he was thinking of the Nazis," Theron said. "But I suppose this is a bit overwhelming, and certainly merciless."

She seemed to ponder.

"You're rather erudite," she said, "for a leisure officer. I don't remember Arthur ever quoting Freud."

"An acquaintance with psychology," I said, covering myself as best I could, "is indeed part of our training. But perhaps Arthur wasn't that interested in that side of our work."

I had no idea if this was true, yet it seemed reasonable enough.

"Could life survive out there now?" I asked, changing the subject.

"Yes. It can and it does, oddly enough. There are some rather interesting plants here. As far as we know, they're on some sort of methane-based cycle, although no one has ever studied them closely. I've been meaning to, actually, because they're not going to be around much longer."

"They're dying?"

"Well, they're very hardy. They had to be, to survive even this long. We thought the nuclear winter would finish them off, but they're still hanging on for the moment. But if the cold doesn't get them—and this is freezing for them compared to what it was like here before—the oxygen will finish them off in the end. Part of our agenda today, in fact, is to collect some plant samples to see how well they're coping. It's to meet a routine reporting requirement for the SA's environmental branch, as if they really care."

"What about something else?" I asked. "Besides the plants. Something we have failed to take note of. Possibly intelligent."

"Have you been talking to Norman Remus?"

"Why do you ask that?"

"Because he asked me the same thing."

"It's a natural question," I said.

"Quite unnatural, I would have thought. Surely you were briefed on the survey? All of us were, including Remus. It's very clear. There's nothing here but the vegetation."

"What about Arthur Duggan?"

"What about him?"

"Did he ever ask you the same question? About intelligent life on Gehenna?"

"You do ask a lot of questions, Mr. Lewin. I don't seem to recall him asking me that. I think I would recall if he had. Arthur rarely showed much interest in my work."

She hesitated then, as if recalling something more.

"Now that you mention it," she said, almost reluctantly, "I do remember him dropping by my lab one day and pestering me with questions about the flora. But he never asked me about any other form of life. And that was the only occasion on which I detected in him any great interest in exobiology."

"Norman Remus suggested to me that there was more to it than that," I said. "He told me that Arthur Duggan believed there was some form of intelligent life out here, life that we were destroying in the terraforming process."

"Norman Remus, with all due respect to an esteemed colleague, has several screws loose. I don't think you should take Norman's word on what Arthur was thinking. He was my husband, after all. And

though he may have been depressed, I don't believe
that he was crazy."

The groundcar came to a halt.

"Here we are," she said.

18

Through the murk I could see a row of cannisters raised on tripods five meters above the ground. As I watched, robot arms snaked out from our groundcar to retrieve the cannisters and pull them within, then snaked out again to put others in their places.

"Atmosphere samples," Theron said.

Two more robot arms, each ending in drill bits, now projected from the car to burrow into the ground on either side of the car.

"Soil," she said, as they withdrew. "Now if we can just scoop up some plants, we can get the hell out of here."

"You mean we're not getting out of the car?" I asked, not sure whether I was pleased or disappointed.

"Not unless we have to. Although sometimes we do."

I watched as two more arms were extruded, this time with paddle-like scoops.

"This is usually the hard one," she said. "Plant samples."

As the scoops withdrew into the car, a red light began to flicker on the control panel.

"Spilled them," she said. "For a change."

She repeated the sequence. Again the red light flashed.

"One more time," she said.

There was the same result.

She sighed.

"Looks like you get to go outside after all."

She handed me a container and a small shovel.

"Try and dig up an unbroken section of the plant," she told me. "When you get it in here, seal the top tightly, like so." She indicated how to tighten the container. "You go to the left of the car, I'll go right. Alright, close your faceplate."

We activated the faceplates of our atmosphere suits.

"Checking radio," she said, and I heard her clearly within my own helmet.

"Checking," I echoed, and she nodded to indicate that the voice-activated signal was coming through loud and clear.

"I'm going to turn on the car's homing signal," she said.

She flipped a switch on the instrument board of the car. I heard a beeping inside my helmet.

"You hear it?"

I nodded.

"If you lose your sense of direction, this should guide you back to the car. But if you still can't find it, then stay where you are and switch on your distress signal, and I'll come and get you."

She pointed to a control on the wrist of my suit.

"Whatever you do," she said, "don't panic and wander off somewhere. Just stay still and signal."

"I'm not going to panic," I said, irritated.

"Alright. Now, when we get out, just take fifteen paces to the left, get your sample, and come back here."

"No problem," I said. "No problem at all."

But on that score I was wrong.

I took my fifteen paces outward without difficulty. The ground felt surprisingly springy under the heels of my boots. Looking down, I saw that I was walking on what looked like a vast bed of whitish-grey moss. It looked much the same as far as the eye could see, but Theron had told me to go fifteen paces for my sample, and fifteen paces I went.

As I walked, the homing signal beeped reassuringly in my ear. Otherwise, I was cut off from all vestiges of civilization. The murk had closed around the ground-car behind me, and around Theron. All points of reference were gone. I was alone in the enclosed world of my suit, a self-contained universe.

I knelt down and carefully got my shovel under a section of the moss. The plant seemed continuous, but the piece came away without difficulty. I placed it in the container and sealed it in tightly. I was so preoccupied with doing all this properly that for a moment I did not even notice that the homing beep had gone silent.

I felt a tug of fear at my stomach: fought it down.

No problem, I told myself. No problem as long as you don't panic.

I picked up the container and the shovel and turned around.

Fifteen paces. I counted them off carefully and deliberately. Twelve. Thirteen. Fourteen. Fifteen. Sixteen...

When I got to eighteen I stopped and took stock. Obviously I had veered off at an angle. But the car had to be somewhere close by. I walked three paces back, three to the left, six to the right.

I admitted defeat.

"Uh, Theron," I said, straining to keep my voice casual. "I think I have a slight problem."

No reply.

"Theron," I said, voice louder and edgier this time. "I've lost contact with the car. Where are you?"

No reply.

She's gone, I thought wildly. Driven off and left me here to die.

My heart raced in my chest. My inner suit was soaked with sweat. I fought down the impulse to scream.

Calm yourself, I thought. Mechanical failure, is all. My radio is out, and that's why I lost the homing signal. Mechanical failure. A glitch. As McKinley had observed, they happened all the time.

Or had someone made it fail? Was there a saboteur here after all? There was no profit, I decided, in that line of thought. It was time to activate my distress signal.

I pushed the switch on my wrist. I heard nothing in my own helmet, but if my radio was out then that was hardly surprising. Still, I couldn't help but wonder if it was working. Perhaps I had not switched it on correctly. Even if I had, I might be wasting my time anyway, if the distress signal had been sabotaged along with my radio.

It was then, while I was fretting over the switch of my distress signal, that I saw...saw whatever it was that I saw.

The murk began, suddenly, to thin out, to become merely misty. And through the murk, towering high above me, I saw the gigantic figure of a man, a man standing perhaps a klick tall, a gigantic and terrifying man.

It was white, this figure, white streaked with black, like the atmosphere of Gehenna itself. Its outlines were fuzzy, threatening to dissolve at any moment back into the surrounding mists. The features of its enormous face were indistinct. And yet I was convinced that I was looking at the face of Arthur Duggan, recognizable to me from photographs and vids. Further, I could have sworn that his terrible face was smiling.

At the same time as I saw this awful vision, I became aware of the voices ringing in my ears once again, the very same sirens which had called to me in my dreams. But this time I was fully awake.

As the gigantic image of Arthur Duggan faded slowly back into the mists, the voices increased in force. *Join us,* they seemed to say. *Embrace us. Join us, as the other man has already done.*

I felt a mixture of desire and terror. I wanted to strip off my cumbersome atmosphere suit, to roll in the soft and yielding moss, to breathe the sweet air of this planet, to live out my dreams. At the same time, I wanted to scream.

Terror won. I did scream, again and again.

And then the mists closed around the white giant, and the voices were gone, and I was again surrounded by the swirling murk of Gehenna.

I staggered, as though I had been hit by a physical blow. I fell to my knees. With my gloved hands, I tugged at the alien soil of the planet. A clump of moss came away in my hands, and I held it up to my faceplate. Under the light from my helmet I saw a whitish mass, made up of thousands of tiny tendrils.

I felt a great emptiness, a terrible sense of loss. I threw the moss away from me. I began to cry.

A hand gripped me by the shoulder and spun me around. A figure in an atmosphere suit loomed over me. Theron. She put her faceplate up against mine so that her voice would carry through the glass.

"Lewin," she said, her face contorted with anxiety, or perhaps just contempt. "What the hell is the matter with you?"

19

Muller was perturbed to hear of the failure of my suit's radio, and promised to have it investigated. But he was even more perturbed to hear how poorly I had conducted myself in the face of the extremity that had developed, how Theron had found me hardly a dozen paces from the groundcar apparently in the midst of some hysterical fit.

"I'm sure it must have been quite frightening," Muller said, after Theron and I had made our report. "Yet it seems to me that you were never in any real danger, except from your own panic. This only confirms my belief that the outside should remain the province of trained and qualified personnel. I'm afraid there will be no more of these little jaunts for you, Lewin."

I felt humiliated, of course, but I could hardly argue with his assessment of the situation. I had indeed conducted myself poorly out there. It was true that Muller's assessment had been made on the basis of incomplete information. But I was not about to tell him, or anyone else, just how frightening the experience had been. Not that the details of my hallucination could have swayed him in any way, except perhaps to request headquarters for my immediate recall. In his position, at least, that is precisely what I would have done.

"Did you see it?" I had asked Theron, once I had recovered some measure of calm. By that point we had been halfway back to the station.

"See what?"

"The mists seemed to clear. I thought I saw..."

I could not bring myself to complete the sentence.

"The mists do lift, periodically. There's growing atmospheric turbulence. I noted that myself. But what did you see?"

"I don't know. A mountain, perhaps."

"Not a mountain. It's pretty flat around here."

She indicated the map glowing on the control console, the gradients curving only gently upward.

"Whatever you saw," she said, "must have been some trick of the light."

"Yes. That's what it must have been."

And certainly that was what I wanted to believe. In a moment of extreme panic, a trick of the light and my own suggestibility to Remus's nonsensical ravings about the outside had somehow combined to produce that bizarre vision. That was what it had to be. There was no other explanation. No reasonable one, at least.

20

Greta Vichevski was considerably more sympathetic than her husband.

"You have slightly elevated adrenal levels," she told me as she completed the medical examination that Muller had ordered. "But you should calm down soon. Let me give you a sleeping medication in case you find it difficult to sleep."

"That won't be necessary," I said. "I'm fine, really."

"You've had a very upsetting experience," she said. "It makes me shiver just to think of it. Lost on the face of this awful planet."

"I was in no real danger."

"I would never venture outside this station. Indeed, sometimes I wonder whether I should even be here."

Norman Remus had said much the same thing, at my first meal here. Yet I was surprised to hear Vichevski make such a remark.

"Why not? Why should you not be here?"

"Oh, not just me. Why are any of us here? In a place like this?"

"You mean, why are we working for the company? I suppose we all had different reasons for that choice..."

"No. That's not the question I'm asking at all. Why is the company here?"

"To terraform this planet," I said, bewildered. "To create a new habitat for humanity, and in the process, hopefully, to achieve an adequate return on its investment."

"Still, there may be some places that we do not belong."

"You almost sound like a Contractionist."

"I have worked for this company for fifteen solars, my husband even longer. I could hardly be a Contractionist. Of course I support the colonization of suitable worlds. I am suggesting only that we should have passed this particular planet by. It is by far the least hospitable planet to which I have ever been assigned."

"But not forever," I pointed out. "Ultimately, through our efforts here, Gehenna will become, as you say, suitable. We are remaking it, reshaping it, to our own requirements."

"And yet there are so many worlds. I can think of no rational reason why we should have picked on this one."

"I disagree. This project can only be completely rational and thoroughly cost-effective. Otherwise, the company would hardly have embarked upon it."

"I am not much interested in the rationale of accountants. And in any case, I believe there was disagreement even on that score. Some thought the commitment of such enormous resources to this project to be complete folly.''

"There will always be those who are lacking in vision. In this case, fortunately, their views failed to carry the day.''

"Or unfortunately.''

"But don't you see that we could hardly let a place like this defeat us? Its very existence is an affront, an affront to our conquest of nature. How could we pass it by? We could not permit such a failure of nerve, we have come much too far for that. We can only go forward. Otherwise . . .''

I realized that I was shouting. I was becoming far too emotional about this. Vichevski's mild speculations were disturbing me out of all proportion to their real significance. Clearly I was still reacting to my brief and terrifying experience outside.

"Otherwise?''

"Otherwise the whole thing would be meaningless,'' I concluded, more quietly. "Don't you see that?''

She laughed.

"What nonsense,'' she said, pleasantly enough. "The kind of nonsense only a certain sort of man would talk.''

"What kind of man?''

"Oh, an intellectual who styles himself a man of action. Like yourself, for example, so eager to participate in our glorious conquest of the universe. That sort of man. Certainly, a woman would never say such a thing.''

I avoided addressing her characterization of me. It was perhaps uncomfortably close to the truth.

"You are suggesting," I said, "that men and women view these things differently? That's a rather old-fashioned idea."

"I believe it's true all the same. I believe that women, at least, know that many things are meaningful, beyond our war with this hapless planet, this vast and inexhaustible adversary of a universe. More meaningful, in some ways."

"For example?" I asked, although I knew quite well what she would say. Some things are dismally predictable.

"Oh, living. Loving. Taking care of one another. Building a better world for our descendants."

I knew better than to try and argue with such sentiments. I would quickly become enmeshed in a damp and clinging fog of sentimentality. I tried to find the higher ground.

"These are basic human urges, of course," I said. "Yet surely more basic still is our urge to control nature. To achieve some predictability in lives once at the mercy of arbitrary and inhuman forces. Should we not build houses against the storms, or plant seeds to ensure our food supply? From the first farmers..."

"Yes, yes," she said impatiently. "Of course we cannot turn back now. But how much further should we go? Where is this leading us?"

"To our destiny," I said. "Whatever that may be."

"To madness," she said. "To the complete abolition of the natural environment. Either we shall succeed in our efforts, succeed in creating an artificial stability as predictable as the tides of the earth or the rising of the sun, and in the process drive ourselves mad with boredom and futility, for what place would we have in such a universe? Or, more likely, we shall fail, and in the process destroy more than just ourselves.''

''And yet we are doing here precisely what you would have us do. Building a better world.''

''We're destroying. Have you seen the vids of this planet from space, taken by the original exploration team? Before we set off those bombs? It was a beautiful planet then, beautiful and terrible. A wonderful and terrible whiteness. Only forty years ago, hardly a flicker of time in the life of this planet. And the exploration team went home with their vids and their soil samples and their dreams. And when they could no longer bear the memory of it, they came back here to destroy it.''

''That's a matter of perspective.''

''We're destroying it,'' she said, firmly. ''Destroying it in order to build...what? Open pit mines. High rise warrens for the miners. Shopping malls, perhaps. Oh, we're destroying it, alright. And we know it, all of us. Even Franz. Although of course he will not admit it.''

''He does not, I take it, agree with your views?''

''Franz, as I have said, is a good company man. And there is a certain honor in that, of course. But he knows I am right all the same. I see him at night, tossing and turning in our bed. Incidentally, how do you sleep, Mr. Lewin? Not well, I would think.''

"I sleep perfectly well," I lied. "My conscience is clear. And speaking personally, I would like nothing better than to destroy that murk out there, obliterate it utterly. When that is done, my sleep will be all the sounder."

"You sound like R. G. Spooner himself."

"I have considerable admiration for R. G. Spooner. I believe he may be the most important human being of our era. Certainly, his achievements are often undervalued."

"Not by the markets," Vichevski said, laughing. "I myself hold several thousand preferred shares of Spooner Interplanetary within the employee savings plan, and I have no complaints about their performance. Franz and I could retire tomorrow, and sometimes I think we should, although Franz, of course, would be at a complete loss if we did so."

"I hold such shares too, although I have not had time to accumulate as many as you. The successful completion of this project will further enhance their value."

"As its failure could cut it in half. But of course there is more at stake here for Mr. Spooner than money. I do not believe, in fact, that he cares much for money at all, except as a means of financing these ever more gargantuan enterprises. In any case, yes, I do indeed admire Mr. Spooner. But not without reservation."

I rose to leave her surgery.

"By the way," she said, as I was making my way toward the door. "You know who led that first exploration team to Gehenna, forty years ago?"

"No. I don't." Although now I could guess.

"R. G. Spooner himself. His very last exploration mission. Afterward the bankers and the shareholders insisted that he stay home. He was too valuable to risk, they said. He could not continue to leave pieces of himself scattered around the universe. A left hand, alright, that was no big deal. But supposing it had been his right hand, the one he used to sign his checks? Or his brain, that vast, cool thinking machine of his? Or even his very will, his will to bring this universe to heel?"

"He lost his hand on Gehenna?"

"Nowhere else."

21

"You're acting like a jerk," my sometime friend Ben Sanders had once told me. "Your department denies your application for tenure, so you run away to outer space. That'll really show them, right?"

He took a swig of beer.

"I'm not trying to show anyone anything..."

"You're acting like a kid. Except you've got a kid yourself."

"I'm not going to be away all the time. Sure, I'm going to miss him. But lots of people travel on business. My father did. He was away for weeks at a time, sometimes."

"He wasn't in outer space."

"He might as well have been. Look, Rosemary understands. This is something I have to do."

"Apply to another university. You'll get tenure somewhere eventually."

"You're missing the point. I don't want to teach anymore. I want to go out there."

"But what's out there?"

"What's here?" I asked, gesturing to take in our surroundings.

We were drinking in a bar which catered largely to the permies. The prices reflected that, which made it a popular watering hole for impoverished teachers and students as well.

"There's nothing here," I said, answering my own question. "Earth is dead. Finished. There are no jobs, no hope. All the action is off-planet now. That's the way it's been going for fifty years, and I want to be a part of it."

"It was the corporations that took the jobs off-planet. And from what I hear, your R. G. Spooner Interplanetary is the worst of them all. Draining money and jobs from Earth, destroying whole environments, ravaging and pillaging wherever they go."

Sanders was far too lazy to be an active Contractionist, and political activism had in any case become a dangerous luxury for university professors. But his reflexive distaste for the big interplanetary development corporations, his thoughtless echoing of the Contractionist line, were common enough on campus. I myself had mouthed similar nonsense at one time.

"Spooner is no worse than any other," I said, "and probably better than some. Look, I don't say the development corporations are perfect. But they are performing a crucial function. If you can look at this historically, they're acting as the instrument of our destiny."

"Which is?"

"To go out into space, where we belong. That's how I see it, anyway. That's where we're going, and the corporations are taking us there. Maybe there were other ways we could have got there, but not as fast or as efficiently. You don't have to love them to see that.

It's an evolutionary process, and there's no way to stop it now. I don't want to stop it, personally. I want to be a part of it."

"Personally, I'd rather be a permie."

I was tempted to point out that Sanders, as a professor of American literature, would hardly be in great demand in space anyway. But instead I looked around the bar at the permies, drinking their beer, watching the widescreen vidshow, playing various electronic games, enjoying their enforced leisure with a kind of grim determination. Actually it was hard to tell the permies from the teachers.

"Ask them if they'd want to go out," I said. "Ten to one they'll say yes. You should see how many applications the corporations get."

"Isn't that the point? There are no jobs here but there are no jobs out there, either. The space corporations have wrecked the entire economy."

"That was happening before space development even began. But sure, there aren't many jobs right now, except for some highly skilled positions. But there will be more, once the development projects move into full swing. And already the wealth from space development is helping to keep the dole payments flowing."

"I can't argue with you. It's as if someone's brainwashed you. Maybe you've brainwashed yourself. If you want to work for a fascist like R. G. Spooner..."

"He's just a businessman," I said, irritated. "An extreme individualist, maybe. How can you call him a fascist?"

"He gives me the creeps. I saw him once on the vids, with that creepy mechanical hand of his. I mean, why doesn't he get one in a fleshtone, at the very least?"

"You don't like his hand. I'm sure he'll be very upset."

"He was talking about *will*. Talking in this very flat and cold and creepy voice. It's just a matter of will, he said, of setting yourself a program and then turning yourself into the instrument of your own will to achieve it."

"Sounds reasonable enough to me."

"You should have heard him, though, the way he said it. I mean, the guy is nuts. He's engaged in this tremendous enterprise, of exploring and conquering the universe, and yet he's deliberately extinguished any flicker of imagination he might once have had, if he had any imagination in the first place. You write yourself your program, and then you pursue it to its solution, no matter what happens."

"But that solution happens to be a very desirable one for all of us."

"Maybe yes, maybe no. But the point is, you may well talk about helping humanity progress, and all of that good stuff; you may even think it. I'm sure Spooner does. But for him it's just an abstraction; it's all an abstraction. He's driving forward on pure intellect."

"And that makes him a fascist?"

"There are some classic points of resemblance. That ability to drive yourself on like some kind of machine. You know, I bet he would rather be a machine than a man. I bet he wishes that all of him was like that hand of his. He shakes hands with his left hand, did you know that? Even though he's right-handed. It's as if anything remotely human or organic revolts him.''

"I didn't know that. You seem to have made quite a study of R. G. Spooner."

"I found him fascinating. Fascinatingly creepy. Did you ever get a close look in his eyes? You can see what a crazy old fucker he is."

"His eyes. Sure, Ben. Sure."

"OK," he said. "Go work for R. G. Spooner. Go conquer the universe with him. Be a jerk. Do whatever you like."

He finished his drink.

"I've got a paper to finish," he said.

Tenured or not, Sanders still had to meet a certain quota of publications to retain his job. Currently, it seemed, he was working on the question of whether Captain Ahab had lost his left or his right leg. Previous exhaustive scholarship had failed to answer this question, but Sanders believed he had a new angle on it.

22

After leaving Vichevski, I accessed the authorized biography of the founder of our company. The text was twenty years old and had never been revised, yet it told me what I wanted to know.

It was as Vichevski had said. In the early days of interstellar development, Spooner had personally led the company's exploration missions, staking claims to dozens of planets and gathering the geophysical evidence necessary to raise capital back on Earth to exploit the wealth of these brand new worlds.

This much I had known, if rather vaguely, before; just as I had known, or assumed, that Spooner had lost his hand in these buccaneering early days. I had not known that he had lost it on Gehenna. It was Spooner who first discovered this world, Spooner who had staked the company's claim, and Spooner who had given it its name.

It had been the very last stop on a tour that had taken in ten worlds before, all more promising than Gehenna. It was the furthest out from Earth that an exploration team had ever gone, and for many years it would remain so. Spooner's crew, exhausted from their labors, homesick for Earth after more than two years off-planet and appalled by the conditions below, had balked at making a landing. The surface temperature was barely survivable, even for their most rugged equipment, and the atmosphere unpromising.

Yet such was the force of Spooner's personality, and such was the loyalty he could command from his crew, that he indeed raised a party of volunteers to make the descent. Spooner, naturally, took the lead.

The exploration party landed and erected a temporary shelter from the heat and the inimical atmosphere. They sent out robot probes to test for mineral content, and they voyaged outward themselves. Spooner, who would ask no man or woman to risk dangers he would not risk himself, led these expeditions into the great whiteness that was then Gehenna.

On one such expedition there was an accident. A crewman was trapped by a rockfall. Spooner, the only crew member close at hand, freed him, tearing away the rocks with his bare hands. Literally so, in the end. So heroic were Spooner's labors, and so arduous the task, that he did not notice the tiny rip in the left glove of his suit. The corrosive atmosphere and the erosive rocks combined to open up a flaw in a fabric never designed for such concentrated punishment.

The crewman was saved, but the hand was so terribly damaged that it had to be amputated.

And so R. G. Spooner returned to Earth. And there he raised the capital to develop the worlds he had found and to build a vast corporate empire.

Gehenna did not figure high on his development agenda, even though the mineral assays had been more than promising. Gehenna was too far out, and its conditions far too hostile, to warrant immediate development. First Spooner had to satisfy his investors with the easier pickings.

"We'll get to it, in the end," Spooner had told his biographer, twenty years ago. "Don't you worry about that. We'll figure out how to handle it. You see, I have a score or two to settle there."

I turned off the terminal.

Was that all it amounted to? Was our presence here due to nothing but an old man's vendetta against the world that had crippled him? Was Spooner really the dangerously obsessed madman that so many already believed him to be?

It was too simple an explanation for my taste. There was more involved here. Something, after all, had persuaded Spooner to drag his weary and complaining crew down here in the first place. The whiteness, the beautiful and terrible whiteness. He could not ignore it. And neither could he leave it be.

Perhaps, in his place, I would not have done the same thing. Yet surely I would have wanted to.

Even now, I could find no fault in his program. We were, I was as convinced as ever, doing the right thing here.

I lay back on my bed and listened to the reassuring throb of the station, the humming of the machines that would finally destroy the wretched atmosphere of this world, blot out forever that whiteness.

23

My little excursion into the history of this planet was all very interesting, but it seemed to bring me no closer to an understanding of my problems here.

At best, it had helped divert me for a moment or two from thinking about my unfortunate and embarrassing little outing. Far from conquering my fear of the world outside this station, my efforts had served only to deepen my anxieties and make an idiot of myself in the eyes of the station's crew. And my unaccountable vision of the gigantic dead man could only lead me to doubt my own sanity.

To top all this off, I had to contend with Charlotte McKinley, who came uninvited to my quarters in an irritatingly playful mood.

"You must be close to finding the killer," she said. "I hear he tried to kill you. Or she."

"There is no killer," I said wearily. "You persuaded me. The case is closed."

"So they succeeded in scaring you off."

"The joke wears thin. I don't want to play detective anymore. I'm really not in the mood. There was a minor mechanical failure, and I panicked. That's all."

"But as Norm might say, why did it fail just then? Perhaps Theron is our saboteur. She had the opportunity."

"Theron rescued me," I said, getting sucked in despite myself.

"Her nerve must have failed. Or perhaps she was only trying to scare you off."

"Enough. Really. I don't want to play anymore. I'm too tired for this. Sad to say, I'm just a plain old leisure officer."

"Of course you are," she said. She pulled a sheaf of papers from the pocket of her jacket and began to read. *"Social interaction in this station is so atomized as to permit virtually any act to go unobserved. Although on the face of it unlikely, one cannot entirely discount the possibility that Arthur Duggan was disposed of in some way. The excessive morbidity of techperson Norman Remus...."*

She was reading from my own notes.

"Where did you get those?"

"I printed them off your terminal," she said. "While you were out having your great adventure, I was playing detective myself. And what are you playing?"

"Those notes were encrypted."

"You didn't use a very sophisticated program. Any halfway decent programmer could crack it. I'm a programmer myself, remember? Even if what I usually program is roast beef and potatoes."

I sighed. Haines, having been proved correct, would no doubt be delighted. My cover was blown. Yet perhaps I could still salvage something from this situation.

"If I tell you," I said, "can I rely on your discretion?"

"I can be discreet," she said, "if necessary."

"It is necessary. We have a complex situation here, and my investigation is by no means complete."

"Then you are a detective after all?"

"Not quite. I'm a psychologist. In the investigative field services group. The company sent me out to check on the situation, morale-wise."

"And how is the situation?"

"I don't think you really need my prognosis on that."

"Will you close down the station?"

She was quick, alright.

"I have reached no conclusion as yet, but that would be a fairly extreme step. More likely we would replace the crew."

"All of us?"

"Not necessarily. Perhaps only one or two members, to achieve a better balance here. After all, there's no reason why individuals who are still performing well should be penalized."

"But you do think the problem is in the crew?"

"Of course. Where else would it be?"

"Where else?" She paused then. "I suppose this means you're going to pull Norm out?"

"It's likely," I admitted.

"So I would be pulled out, too?"

"Not necessarily. Obviously I can't promise anything, but if you were to assist me by keeping this to yourself for the time being, I would be extremely grateful. I could strongly recommend that you be allowed to stay on. Assuming that you wanted to stay, of course.''

''I do want to stay. And, yes, I will be discreet.''

She shook her head.

''Poor Norm,'' she said. ''He was such a nice man, once, and then he just got crazier and crazier.''

''I had another conversation with him the other day. Much weirder than the first one. About the outside. He seems to think there is something out there. Something living.''

''He told you, too? He used at least to have the sense to keep his mouth shut about that with the others. Although I can't say I really want to hear about it, either. It's as I said. Crazier and crazier.''

''Norm also suggested to me that the late Arthur Duggan shared the same belief—that there was something out there. Do you suppose that could be true?''

''Arthur?'' She seemed surprised. ''He never mentioned that to me. But then Arthur was always a rather private sort of person, for all his apparent gregariousness, and toward the end he hardly talked at all.''

I wanted, then, to tell her about my own experience outside that day. But I was not sure that she was the best person in whom to confide, no matter how much I needed to talk about it.

''Is this important?'' she asked. ''Do you think there really could be something outside? Surely that's impossible?''

''Yet perhaps Arthur Duggan experienced something all the same,'' I said thoughtfully. ''Something that only seemed to originate outside the station, but actually was arranged from within.''

''How?''

''Drugs, perhaps. A mild hallucinogen, combined with some sort of suggestion.''

''Or a dream machine. Greta has one in her surgery. I've borrowed it from time to time, to help me sleep.''

I had heard of such a device, but never seen one. It was a relatively new therapeutic tool, used primarily in the treatment of insomnia. It induced carefully programmed dreams of a pleasant and non-threatening nature.

''A good point,'' I said. ''Someone could have used their own program.''

In fact, I thought, someone could have been using it on me.

''You see,'' she said, ''every detective needs an assistant.''

She turned to me and tilted her head back expectantly. It was then that I departed from normal procedures for the second time that night. I could offer some very good reasons for what I did, but in all honesty I would have found it very difficult to do anything else. I was a long way from home, further than I had ever been before, and normal procedures were a long way from my mind.

Later, however, after McKinley had returned to her own quarters following several hours of unscheduled and exhausting but not uncreative or unpleasurable leisure activities, I was able to review the situation with considerable satisfaction.

Clearly, things had not gone exactly as planned. But then, matters here were rather more complex than I had originally anticipated, and clinging to past techniques would have demonstrated only an excessive rigidity. In retrospect, in fact, I was able to congratulate myself on my improvisations. McKinley might yet prove a useful ally in my investigation, if she could be trusted—a question on which I had as yet reached no conclusion.

24

At first-meal the next day Muller had strange and disturbing news.

"I have received a communication from headquarters," he told us. "It seems we may expect a visitor imminently."

Given the logistic complexities and vast expenses of space travel, it was quite unusual for an isolated station like this one to receive a visitor at all. Under normal circumstances, an entire tour might elapse without the crew's ever seeing another human being, except on a screen via dirac communication.

"An SA inspector?" Theron asked.

It seemed unlikely. Given sufficient provocation, it was true, the Space Administration, a largely toothless bureaucracy leaning heavily on the side of the development companies, would on occasion dispatch one of its regional inspectors. But the SA had as yet no reason to show such an interest in Gehenna.

"No," Muller said. "From the company."

He paused here, as if unsure how to confide his news.

"Do you want us to guess?" Remus asked. "Has leisure officer Lewin enlisted your cooperation in a game of twenty questions?"

"R. G. Spooner," Muller said. "R. G. Spooner is coming here."

"R. G. Spooner?" repeated Vichevski, clearly as surprised at this news as the rest of us. "But that's incredible. R. G. Spooner never leaves Earth."

"Apparently he does, now," Muller said. "He has recently embarked on a three-month-long tour of his company's development sites. We should remember that Mr. Spooner no longer runs the company on a day-to-day basis. His presence on Earth is no longer mandatory."

"He left Ron Jr. in charge?" I asked.

"As I understand it," Muller said, rather frostily, "Mr. Ronald C. Spooner is accompanying his father on this tour. To the best of my knowledge, Elmer Crantz remains president and chief operating officer of the company. But perhaps you have more recent information than I."

Elmer Crantz was married to Spooner's eldest daughter. He was widely regarded as a straw man, although it was not clear whose straw man he was.

"An old man's last wish," said Vichevski. "To revisit his ancient haunts. Perhaps there is an ounce of sentiment in him after all."

"It's not our place to speculate on his motives," Muller said, rather sharply. "If all goes according to plan, Mr. Spooner will be arriving here next week. Gehenna, in fact, will be only the second stop on his tour. I'm sure you all know that he has taken a personal interest in this project."

"He'll be staying over?" McKinley asked.

"I would not imagine so," Muller said. "I would think that any visit would be a brief one. Yet we must prepare for all contingencies."

He looked around the table.

"Things have been somewhat slipshod here of late. It is true that I have accepted this situation, hoping that in time matters would correct themselves. I must now insist on a general improvement in performance and attitude. Reports must be brought up to date, maintenance schedules strictly conformed to, and normal procedures obeyed in their every aspect."

He seemed to be looking in particular at Norman Remus. The little techperson avoided his gaze.

"That's all," he said.

There was a brief personal communication from Earth awaiting me on my terminal when I returned to my quarters. It was a dirac letter from my good friend Vince Hendricks, in which he seemed to tell of a recent fishing holiday, and of the big fish and little fish he had caught.

The dirac was in fact from my supervisor, Samuel Haines.

I applied the decoding sequence that would allow me to translate this communication. The message told me essentially what I had just learned from Muller. R. G. Spooner was heading out to gaze upon his handiwork, accompanied by his son.

Neither Spooner nor his son was intimately acquainted with the recent events at Station Gehenna. Ron Jr., as senior manager responsible for human resources, would have been told that a suicide had taken place and that an investigation into morale was being conducted. It was unlikely, however, that he would have informed himself about the situation at any more detailed level.

He might know of my presence here, but probably he did not, although he could always access that information if he required it. So I probably could hope to maintain my cover identity here, although it was possible that Ron Jr. could blow it for me.

The end of the message required no decoding. "Write soon now," Haines told me.

I had as yet filed no report on my investigation. So far I was at a loss as to what to report.

Yet, just as Muller had demanded of us, there would now be a great improvement in my performance and attitude. Or so I resolved.

25

In pursuit of resolving my stalemated investigation, I sought out Valerie Theron in her laboratory. She was hard at work analyzing the samples we had collected the day before.

"Recovered?" she asked drily.

"Oh yes, thank you. I came to apologize for any inconvenience I may have caused you yesterday."

"That's alright. I accept your apology."

She turned back to her workbench, as though to dismiss me.

"How is it?" I asked. "The plant life, that is."

She held up a sealed transparent container, holding vegetation from the outside. A tube leading into the container fed it the noxious fumes to which it was accustomed.

"Degenerating, apparently. Or at least, there is increasing discoloration, and a reduction in the density of the tendrils. There also appears to be some mutation in the genetic structure."

"Radiation damage?"

"I don't think so. The radiation has faded almost to nothing, while this mutation is something new. It's almost as if it was trying, unsuccessfully, to adjust to the higher oxygen content. But I don't have enough data yet to draw any firm conclusion. I simply don't know enough about the life cycle."

I stepped forward to peer into the bottle at the clump of mosslike stuff.

"What are they?"

"It, really. Not they. As far as I can determine, this is the only lifeform here above the microscopic level. There's just this one great big carpet of ground vegetation covering almost this entire planet from wall-to-wall. Except there are no walls. Except around the stations."

"Does it bother you? What we're doing to this moss?"

"I don't take the destruction of any genus lightly. But we can't anthropomorphize. We can't allow ourselves to become excessively sentimental about something as insignificant as this moss."

"Every species for himself."

"Yes," she said. "Himself."

26

After leaving Theron, I paid a visit to Greta Vichevski in her surgery.

"I was not completely honest with you the other day," I said. "The fact is, I have been having a little trouble sleeping."

I suffered the expected knowing smile.

"You see," I continued, "I have had some rather disturbing dreams."

"And you wish to tell me about them?" she asked. "I am no psychiatrist, of course, but I have a working knowledge of the field."

"Not really. I appreciate the offer, of course. It's just that I don't believe in that sort of thing."

"What do you believe in, then? Sleeping medication?"

"If necessary," I said. "Although I would prefer another solution."

"What kind of solution did you have in mind?" she asked. "Warm milk? A bedtime story? A long brisk evening walk?"

"I believe that you are equipped with a dream machine."

"Ah hah. A technological fix, why not indeed? Just the ticket for you, I would say. I do in fact have such a device. Unfortunately I have only the one, and it is currently in use."

"Who has it?" I asked.

"I cannot tell you that, of course," she said. "No more than I could tell what medications I am prescribing. These matters are between doctor and patient."

"Of course."

"Don't look so disappointed. I will see if I can work out some arrangement for you to share the device. I should tell you, though, that it is a rather useless contraption, capable of producing only the dullest dreams."

She pulled a booklet from her desk, paged through it.

"This is a listing of the software available for it. I have only the therapeutic programs, of course. See here."

She handed me the booklet, open at the right page.

RELAXATION DREAMS, I read.
001—A warm summer's day.
002—Swimming
003—Walking in the country
004—Floating
005—Flying
006—Eating ice cream

"Eating ice cream?" I asked.

"Oh, a real winner, that one. I could hardly wait to wake up."

I read on.

"What about the sex dreams?" I asked.

There was a listing of sex dreams, divided into heterosexual and homosexual, and subdivided as to male and female. The titles were not terribly descriptive. "Blonde." "Brunette." "Two Blondes." And so on.

"I can't say I've tried them all. I did run one of them, purely out of professional interest, you understand. It wasn't terribly imaginative, although I suppose it was better than the ice cream. These are therapeutic dreams, after all. If you want steamier stuff, you will have to send away for it. I believe that recreational dreaming is becoming quite an industry back on Earth. Are you feeling sexually frustrated, Mr. Lewin?" she asked. "I ask you this as doctor to patient."

"I wouldn't say that," I said, annoyed at this remark. "Why do you ask? Were you planning to offer some assistance?"

"I was thinking of course of the dreams," Vichevski said. "Since I ought not to prescribe them simply to gratify a purely salacious curiosity, but neither should I deny them to an individual requiring relief. Although as I've told you, these dreams are quite boring things, really, and I'm surprised that Charlotte counselled you to seek them."

"Charlotte?" I said. "I don't know why you say that. I haven't talked to her about this."

"My mistake, then. You must have been discussing something else last night."

I understood, then, her question about my sexual frustration.

"Last night?"

"Rather late last night. Franz was working late, and I was out for a stroll, and I happened to see Charlotte leaving your quarters. But as I said, I was obviously mistaken—you must have been discussing something else."

Clearly, some things in this station did not go unobserved.

"I don't see how that's any of your concern," I said.

"Norman Remus concerns me," she said. "Particularly after losing Arthur Duggan. I would not like to lose another."

"You're suggesting that Remus may be suicidal?"

"I didn't say that. But I do think that Norman is somewhat fragile of late. I would not like to see him upset unnecessarily. But of course, we must live our lives as we think best."

"Yes," I said. "As we think best."

I turned the conversation back to the issue at hand. "These dreams. How do they work?" I asked.

"No magic really. Through a mild but direct electronic stimulation of certain centers in the brain, inducing certain mental states and at the same time encouraging suggestibility to certain scripted aural cues."

She showed me the cover of the brochure. A man with an idiotic expression on his face was lying on a couch. He wore a metal headband on his forehead and earphones on his ears. These were hard-wired to a small box beside the couch, which I assumed to be the dream machine.

"A rather clumsy arrangement," I said.

"Isn't it, though? I suppose in the end we'll be able to transmit the dreams without trussing you up like a turkey. But that is how it works now."

"Could you write your own programs for this?" I asked.

"Devise your own dreams? An interesting idea. Perhaps you could, if you were acquainted with the protocols. It would be a lot of trouble, though."

It was hard to see how anyone could have used this device on me while I was asleep. Surely I would have sensed the physical intrusion involved? And even if this device had been used to disturb my dreams, I did not see how it could have accounted for my waking vision of Arthur Duggan.

Nevertheless, when Vichevski left for mid-meal, I ducked into her surgery and checked her files to see who was currently using the dream machine.

There were only two recorded users: Charlotte McKinley and Valerie Theron. Theron was the current user. She had been in possession of the machine on several occasions. This time around she had been using it since just prior to my arrival at Station Gehenna.

And what dreams was she running? I could not resist looking. She was dreaming of a warm summer day, and of flying, and of floating, and yes, of eating ice cream. She did not dream of sex. I wondered what other arrangements she might have made.

27

To complete my rounds for the day, I sought out Norman Remus. I did so with a distinct lack of enthusiasm. But though it was not a prospect I relished, there was something we needed to talk about. Something formed a common bond between us which I would much rather not have shared.

Remus seemed to have taken Muller's admonishments to heart. I found him alone in the central control room of the station, pouring over the readings coming in from the substations and swearing softly to himself.

"I'm busy," he said, when he became aware of my presence. "There's a glitch at substation three. We're probably going to have to go out there and take a look at it. And I'm still not interested in signing up for any recreational activities, Spooner or no Spooner."

He swivelled in his chair back to the board.

"That's not what I wanted to talk about."

"What is it, then?" he asked, without looking up.

"The outside. I wanted to talk about the outside."

Grudgingly, he turned back toward me, his face betraying no sign of interest. For a moment I thought he might be about to disown entirely his previous ravings, if ravings they were.

"What about it?" he said.

"A few days ago, when we were talking by Airlock Two, you mentioned your feeling that there was something...something living outside the station. Something interested in us."

"Yes?" he asked, still affecting disinterest.

"Yesterday, when I was outside with Theron, I thought I saw...something."

"What sort of something?" he asked, as if bored with this whole conversation.

I realized that our roles had been somehow reversed. Now I was the madman, and he was interrogating me. I did not like the feeling much at all.

"First, you tell me," I said. "Tell me what you have seen."

"Nothing," Remus said. "I have seen nothing at all. You're the one who's seeing things, apparently."

He swivelled back to his control board.

"Alright," I said. "I'll go first. I saw what seemed to be a man. An enormous man."

Remus swivelled back, any pretense of indifference shattered.

"Duggan," he said. "You saw him, too. Jesus Christ."

He told me then that he had glimpsed the same white giant on two occasions now.

"The first time I was out on my own, just checking the station walls, cleaning the outside monitors. You're not supposed to go out on your own, of course, not even that far, but I'd done it before a dozen times. I liked it, you know, getting away from everyone else. This was just a week after Duggan took his little walk, and things were kind of tense in here, so I figured I'd get out for awhile.

"I finished up one set of monitors, and I turned to walk around the wall to the next set. And then I saw him, looming over me. Not five hundred meters away. So big he could have crushed me like an ant, booted the station right off the planet like an overripe melon. A giant, a giant ghost."

"You thought it was a ghost?"

"I didn't really think at all. I just ran to the lock and got back inside the station. And when I looked out he was gone. Vanished back into the mists."

"And you told no one about this?"

"I told Charlotte. She said it was some kind of illusion, some sort of atmospheric formation that I had somehow turned into a man. She said there was no such thing as a ghost, not on Earth and certainly not on Gehenna. And even if there was, whoever heard of a ghost a kilometer tall? She said we were all under some strain, and I should try and take it easy and forget about all this."

"And you accepted that?"

"I wanted to," he said. "She made sense. Although still, in the back of my mind, I knew it was Duggan all the same. But Charlotte was so nice and reasonable about it. And of course, as she pointed out, if I didn't keep my mouth shut, I could get myself sent home. And then she would get sent home, too. And I would probably never work for the company again. They'd fob me off with some disability pension and dump me back among the permies. She couldn't do that, she told me, couldn't go back and be a permie.

She would divorce me first and marry someone else and get reassigned."

I am not a betting man, but I would not have given very good odds that Remus's marriage to McKinley would be renewed at the end of this tour of duty. Clearly, though, he lived in hope.

"So I did try to forget it. But it happened again."

The second time he had been out in the groundcar with Theron a few weeks later, returning from a sample-gathering trip much like the jaunt I had undertaken the previous day. He had seen the gigantic figure of Arthur Duggan through the window of the car. Theron, apparently, saw nothing. That was when he had realized that this was some private phantom of his. The vision had again disappeared. He had held his peace, had sat trembling and sweating in the groundcar all the way back to the station.

"So I told Charlotte again, and we had the same discussion, except this time she didn't persuade me at all. This time I decided it really had to be a ghost. I mean, I know it sounds crazy now, but I thought, what else could it be? We all knew there was nothing living on this planet except us and the moss, right? So it had to be a ghost. But what did he want with me? Why was he haunting *me*? What did I ever do to him? The guy offed himself, after all.

"But then I started to think, maybe he didn't. Maybe someone killed him. Maybe he's trying to tell me that. And I realized that there had been something about his death that bothered me all along. So I pulled the specs on the door circuits, and found out the stuff I told you, about the safety program."

"Why would Duggan's ghost . . ." I was fully aware of the absurdity of this conversation, yet I seemed to have no choice but to pursue it to its ultimate conclusion. "Why would he ask your help? You weren't exactly friends, after all."

"Not exactly, no."

"A ghost," I said carefully, "is sometimes thought of as a symbol of guilt."

"You think I don't know that? I mean, at first I thought, maybe he's somehow got the wrong guy here, maybe he thinks *I* killed him. And then I started to think, maybe he's right, maybe I did kill him and now I've forgotten all about it. You know, like some psycho on the vids. Or maybe there is no ghost at all and this is all some weird guilt-ridden projection from inside my head, maybe I'm haunting myself for some crime I don't even remember. I imagine a psychologist might say that."

I was momentarily startled. But clearly he was not referring to me. Charlotte had kept my secret, at least for the moment.

"I couldn't be absolutely sure that wasn't true until just now, when you told me you saw the same thing. I couldn't rule out the possibility that I had killed Duggan, and that this was all just some personal delusion of mine. I didn't really believe it, of course. I mean, I think I would know if I killed Duggan. But I knew somebody did; I was able to prove that much.

"Oh, I've had all kinds of crazy thoughts. You can't imagine what I've gone through."

"But did you really prove he was killed? I hear that Muller was able to account for the failure of the safety program quite convincingly."

"Muller is covering his ass," Remus said. "And maybe someone else's too. And don't you think I'm afraid to tell old R. G. that."

"You're going to tell R. G. Spooner all this?" I asked.

"Yes, I am. All of it. You know, I was thinking of sending him a dirac, but I knew it would never get through to him. But what do you know, he's coming here. So I'm going to tell him. And then they can go right ahead and recall me, if they like. In fact, right now I think I'd rather be a permie than stick around here."

"It might sound a little strange," I said. "Especially the part about the ghost."

"It isn't a ghost," Remus said. "I realize that now. I just wasn't thinking very clearly then."

"Then what is it?"

"You know what it is. That's why you came to me. You know it's something outside this station. I didn't put it together until later, when I remembered how Duggan would spend so much time just staring outside. I realized that it wasn't a ghost, it was just some little show they arranged for me. And for you, too, now."

"They?"

"The things outside. The things Duggan saw, in some other shape, Christ knows what. Maybe he saw himself."

He covered his face with his hands.

"And then again," he said, "maybe it is Duggan. Duggan horribly changed. Duggan after joining them, merging with them, somehow. I don't know."

"But there's nothing out there," I said. "It's just impossible."

"I know what I saw. I know what I've felt. There's something out there, alright. Maybe it's the moss. Maybe it's something else, something we don't know about. We've hardly scratched the surface of this planet. Maybe somehow it's the whole goddamned planet."

"Come on. A living planet?"

"I know," Remus said. "Comic book stuff, right? But what do we really know about planets? What do we really know about anything, except how to tear it apart? Look, what difference does it make what it is? The point is, there's something out there. You know it, I know it, I think everyone in this station knows it although they'd rather die than admit it, which maybe they will..."

It was at that moment that Muller lumbered into the control room and threw an interested glance in my direction.

"No," Remus said, in a loud voice. "Can't make the bridge game tonight. Got a lot of work to do around here."

And to me, more quietly, "We'll discuss this later."

But we never would.

28

That afternoon, Muller and Remus left the station in a flyer for substation three, a six-hour flight away, to check on certain malfunctioning systems. Valerie Theron would act as station commander in Muller's absence.

I had cancelled all formal leisure activities for the remainder of the week in any case, to give the crew time to prepare for Spooner's visitation. It was perhaps an even greater relief to me than it was to them. Nonetheless I was hard at work at my terminal, well into the evening, developing grandiose recreational programs stretching two solars into the future, on the remote chance that Spooner would wish to inspect them. It was a relief to know that I would never have to execute them.

Around 2200 hours Charlotte McKinley arrived at my quarters.

"There's something you ought to take a look at."

She led me directly to Valerie Theron's laboratory.

"She isn't here," she said, as I hesitated at the door. "She's down in the control room communicating with Muller."

The door was locked. McKinley produced a small terminal from her pocket and communicated rapidly with the door circuit. The door swung open.

"Neat," I said.

"Simple really," she said. "Maybe I should have been the detective."

The laboratory was as I remembered it from that morning. I had seen nothing suspicious then and I saw nothing now. But McKinley led me to another door at the back of the room, this one also locked. She repeated the same procedure with her pocket terminal, and I found myself looking into a storage cupboard, the shelves crammed with equipment.

"There," she said, pointing to the highest shelf.

I recognized the dream machine that I had seen in the picture on the brochure in Vichevski's office. Yet it did not look quite the same. The headphones and headband had been removed. Something else had been attached: a small box with a cone-like projection.

I took it down and set it on the workbench.

"She's been making some modifications," I said. "But what does it do?"

In answer McKinley reached over and flipped a switch. Lights glowed, as power flowed from a built-in cell. She flipped another switch.

I was five years old, and I was eating an ice cream cone. Vanilla, my favorite flavor. It was the best ice cream cone I had ever tasted. The hot summer sun beat down on me and my ice cream cone, and little rivulets of melted ice cream ran down my fingers. I licked them off and attacked the cone itself. It was such a creamy, smooth ice cream cone, so cool, so right, I hoped it would never end ...

And then, abruptly, I was back in the laboratory. I looked at my hands. No ice cream cone.

"What the hell was that?"

"I think this must be Theron's personal research project," McKinley said.

"Dream projection. No wires, no cables, no sleep, even. She's going to be a very rich lady."

"Isn't that missing the point a little?"

I knew what point she was referring to. I didn't like it very much.

"What other kind of dreams does she have there?" I asked. "Apart from ice cream?"

Sirens serenading me across the plains of moss, perhaps. Or gigantic white ghosts.

"I checked before," McKinley said, indicating the box of diskettes. "Just standard stuff. A warm summer's day. Waves. Sitting on a train. Like that. She must keep the good stuff somewhere else."

"The good stuff?"

"The stuff she's been using on Norm. And I guess on Arthur, too."

"Maybe we're jumping to conclusions here," I said. "Maybe this really is just some pure research project."

"The great detective," she said. "You've found your saboteur, and now you're not willing to admit it."

"Perhaps we should confront her with this. Give her a chance to explain what it's for."

"And you think she's going to admit it? That she's been trying to drive people crazy?"

"No," I said. "I suppose not. I guess the thing to do is to take this to Muller, lay the whole thing out for him. I can't say I'm keen to do that, but I don't see any other alternative."

"Muller isn't here," McKinley said. "Even when he comes back, I'm not sure we should take this to him. Not yet, anyway. I've often wondered if he and Theron were involved, somehow. Certainly he has a soft spot for her, putting up with Arthur so long. We may need more than this to convince him."

"How much more?" I asked. "Maybe we could search her quarters for the other stuff. Or somehow catch her in the act..."

Consideration of this question, however, would have to be postponed. For it was at that moment that Valerie Theron's voice boomed out over the intercom.

"All staff members to the control room," she said. "We have an emergency condition here."

Hurriedly, we replaced the machine on its shelf, locked the doors behind us, and responded to her summons.

29

Vichevski arrived almost simultaneously with us. Theron was at the communications board. She rose to greet us.

"We have a potentially serious situation," she said, without preliminary. "I must ask you, Dr. Vichevski, and you, Mr. Lewin, to accompany me.

She turned to McKinley.

"You," she said, "will remain here to mind the store. You know how to work the board?"

McKinley nodded.

"But what is the emergency?" Vichevski asked. "What has happened? Has something happened to Franz?"

"Yes," Theron said. "There has been an accident involving the commander and techperson Remus. At this point in time, we don't know how serious an accident."

"But what happened?" Vichevski asked, again.

"We shouldn't waste time," Theron said. "I'll explain on the way."

We rushed to the main airlock and embarked in one of the flyers in the vehicle bay. Theron sent the signal to open the roof, then punched in the program to substation three. As the flyer shot upward into the skies of Gehenna, she explained the situation.

Muller and Remus had arrived at the substation without incident around 1900 hours. They had checked on an apparent operational defect in the fractionation equipment, finding no mechanical problem. In communication with Theron, they had subsequently located the fault in the messaging software linking the main computer with the one in the substation. All this had taken only a couple of hours.

"Rather than sleep over in the substation," Theron said, "Commander Muller decided he wanted to come back, catching some sleep in the flyer. These substations are pretty gloomy places, and he had a lot more he wanted to do here before Mr. Spooner arrived."

They had started their return journey at 2230 hours, and promptly dropped out of normal radio contact.

"The flyer is supposed to transmit a constant signal while in the air, which is monitored by the main computer here. A few minutes after they took off, an alarm sounded, indicating loss of contact. I tried to reach them, but without success."

"They've vanished?" Vichevski asked.

"Not entirely." She pointed to the map on the control panel, where a spot was glowing red. "We are getting a distress signal from the flyer, here. About fifty klicks from substation three, although quite off-course."

"So they're alive?" Vichevski asked.

"I certainly hope so," Theron said. "But I cannot say that for sure. The distress signal is a fully automated system, separate from the radio, and designed to withstand considerable punishment. It might operate even if the entire flyer disintegrated around it."

The distress on Vichevski's face was evident.

"But of course, there's no reason to believe it has," Theron said quickly. "These flyers are quite sturdy."

"They have withstood emergency landings before?" I asked.

"No," she said. "In theory, there is no reason why they should not. But there has never been such an accident on Gehenna before. In other places, yes. But Gehenna is not like other places."

"So we're going to try to land there?" I asked, indicating the spot on the map.

"No," she said. "We will proceed to substation three and cover the remaining distance by groundcar."

"But that will take much longer," I objected. "They could die there, waiting for us."

A few minutes before, I had had great difficulty in picturing Valerie Theron as a saboteur. Now, suddenly, I wondered whether she was deliberately delaying our arrival, whether in fact she might have been responsible for the accident to Muller's flyer in the first place.

"I am fully aware of the need to hurry," she said icily.

"Then why not land the flyer?"

"As acting station commander I am under no obligation to explain my actions to you. It is up to me to make these decisions, and up to you to help me implement them."

Now Vichevski spoke up, too.

"But surely it would be quicker, Valerie."

"A quick death, perhaps. For your sake, Greta, rather than his, let me tell you that I have of course considered the idea of attempting to land the flyer. I find it too risky."

She explained, then, that these flyers were designed only to be guided by automated systems between the stations. It would be extremely dangerous to attempt a manual landing.

"I must first of all consider the safety of my own crew," she said. "In any case, it would hardly help the commander and techperson Remus if we were to crash ourselves in the attempt to rescue them."

I remained suspicious, but I could find no flaw in her logic.

"How long will it take us to reach them from the substation?" I asked.

"An hour, perhaps. It could be a little longer. We don't have a lot of experience in running the ground-cars over long distances. And the terrain around there is somewhat hillier than around the main station."

I looked at my watch. Less than an hour had elapsed since the flyer had dropped out of radio contact. Theron could not be accused of dragging her feet in responding to the alarm. We would reach them in a little under seven hours from the presumed moment of landing.

"How much oxygen does the flyer hold?" I asked.

"Oxygen is not really the problem," Theron said. "The flyer could sustain two people for several days. The question is one of shelter from the heat. If the flyer remains intact, there is no problem in this regard.''

"And if the flyer cracked open?''

"Then they must rely on the more limited protection of their suits. But even then, their suits should sustain them quite comfortably past our estimated rendezvous time. I say 'should' since this also has never been put to the test. Each suit contains twelve hours of oxygen and is guaranteed to protect against the heat much longer than that. But again, the guarantee has never been tested. None of us has ever ventured out for more than a few hours at a time.''

Vichevski asked the obvious question, one I had already decided not to ask.

"What if the suits were also damaged by the impact of the crash?''

Theron spread out her hands, gloved palms open.

"That's the worst case, of course,'' she said.

She did not need to elaborate.

30

I must have dozed off. I woke with a start as the flyer lurched in the air. Vichevski only half-suppressed a scream of surprise.

"Normal turbulence," Theron said, as calm as ever. "These machines can handle a great deal more punishment than that. There was no reason why one should have crashed."

"Then why did it crash?" I asked.

"Mechanical failure, I suppose."

"Or sabotage," I said.

Both Theron and Vichevski now gave me their full attention.

"What a bizarre thing to suggest," Theron said.

"Yes," Vichevski said. "Why do you say such a thing? What reason do you have to make such a statement?"

"Oh, I don't know," I said. "It just seems to me that we're having a lot of mechanical failures around here. Muller's flyer. My suit radio. The safety program on Airlock Two."

"What safety program?" Vichevski asked.

"The one that should have stopped Arthur Duggan from taking his walk."

"I don't know what you're talking about," Vichevski said.

Ask your husband, I thought of saying, but it did not seem the most appropriate comment under the circumstances.

Unlike Vichevski, Theron did not seem surprised by my comment. Perhaps Muller had involved her in testing the door circuits. Or perhaps she had sabotaged the mechanism herself.

"Machines fail," Theron said. "People fail. Let's not get too melodramatic here."

She dismissed me then, turning to stare fixedly out the window of the flyer, although in fact there was very little to see. It was night out there, and the murk was almost impenetrable, even travelling fifteen klicks above the surface. Once I thought I caught a glimpse of Alpha, the larger of Gehenna's two satellites—invisible from the ground—racing through the sky.

Vichevski sat flipping restlessly through a book, resolutely ignoring the view. It was clear that she was not enjoying this ride, that she was reining in her emotions only by sheer force of will. Theron, on the other hand, appeared as cool and detached as ever.

"I am sorry I had to ask you to come," Theron told her, obviously noting her distress. "But we may need a medical officer."

"Much better to be here than back at the station waiting," Vichevski said. "Although this world terrifies me."

I turned back to the window. Arthur Duggan's bloated face stared back in at me, then flickered away.

"Jesus," I said involuntarily.

"What?" Theron asked. "What's the matter?"

"Did you see . . ." I began. Clearly neither of them had seen. "I thought I saw . . ." I stopped myself.

"Another trick of the light?" Theron asked. "Please try to get a hold of yourself, Mr. Lewin. I had my doubts about asking you to come in the first place, but I thought I might need an extra pair of hands. And I could hardly leave you in the station on your own."

I was not exactly pleased with this assessment of my usefulness to this rescue mission, but I did not try to argue with it. I was still too stunned by what I had just seen.

My elaborate theory of sabotage and dream projectors had fallen apart almost as quickly as I had put it together. There was no projector on board this craft, no way that Theron could have induced that hideous vision.

I would have to find some other explanation. Possibly Remus was right in his speculations about alien lifeforms. Or possibly I was going mad. Not the most dignified fate for a psychological investigative officer.

Disintegration, I thought. The entire crew was disintegrating, and me along with them. Even as the flyer settled down into the landing bay of substation three, I felt a deep sense of foreboding. Only doom, I thought, awaited us on this terrible planet.

31

"No forests on Gehenna," Haines had agreed with me, as we had talked in his office what now seemed like a hundred years ago. "Nor on Fishman's World."

"Fishman's World?" I echoed, puzzled by this remark. I had heard of the place only vaguely. It was certainly not a celebrated case in our records. "That was a plague, wasn't it? Wiped out an agronomy research crew fifteen or twenty years ago?"

"Twelve," Haines said. "But it wasn't a plague that killed them. It was poison. In the meal rations. They all ate it. Eighteen crew members. For obvious reasons, public affairs preferred to call it a plague."

"Murder-suicide?" I asked.

"That was the obvious explanation," Haines said.

"Fishman's World," I said again. "We're not developing that one right now, are we?"

"No," replied Haines. "The SA placed it off-limits."

"Because of a murder-suicide?" I asked. "Isn't that a little extreme? Or did they buy that story about the plague?"

"The SA was fully informed. They agreed to the cover story for their own reasons."

"I don't get it. I mean, sure, it's a grisly story. But it doesn't sound terribly mysterious. It's easy enough to imagine how it went down. One guy develops an obsessive hatred of everyone else, to the point where he can no longer stand living with them. And one day he kills everyone, including himself."

"As I said, that was the obvious explanation," Haines said. "But we were unable to reconstruct any unusual interpersonal conflicts, or any evidence of the potential for such severe emotional disturbance in any crew member."

"You can't always project who's going to blow," I pointed out. "If you could, they wouldn't need us. It had to be the way I described it."

"It could have been suicide."

"Mass suicide? With, what, ten, fifteen people all agreeing to off themselves?"

"Eighteen," Haines said. "They could have. I was unable to rule it out."

"I don't understand why not. And I still don't understand why they declared the planet off-limits."

"It was my recommendation. Management didn't like it, of course, but once I'd filed my report with the SA, they had no choice but to comply."

I understood now why Haines had topped out.

"I still don't get it," I said. "On what grounds did you recommend withdrawal?"

"I filed a PAI," he said.

I had to struggle even to place the term. *Possible Alien Involvement*. You learned about it in field school, but it was of purely academic interest. Certainly I had never heard of anyone actually filing one.

The fact of the matter was that there were no aliens; not, at least, in the sense of a PAI report. Not at any rate on any planet that we or any other development company had as yet surveyed. There were alien planet forms, sure, even the occasional animal. But in almost fifty years of expansion, no one had documented any reason to suspect the existence of any form of alien intelligence.

"Aliens made the crew suicide?" I asked.

"Yes," he said. "Or else they entered the station to poison the meal themselves. Or they took control of one individual in order to achieve that goal. It could have happened any one of those ways. Yet I suspect it was done simply by manipulating the emotions of the crew to create a uniform and suicidal depression. That is how they seemed to influence humans, on an emotional rather than physical level."

"You saw these aliens?"

"No," he said. "I'm not even sure they had any physical presence, at least in any way we would understand it. I did not see them, but I felt them. I believe the research crew felt them, too. There were some circumstantial hints, at least, journal entries and the like. And there were some strange incidents during the period of our investigation."

"But you're telling me that in the end it just came down to a gut feeling? A feeling that you were having an encounter with aliens?"

"I don't know what I had an encounter with," Haines said, suddenly weary of this conversation. "I just know we got the hell out of there as soon as we could, and we never went back."

"And the SA never even tried to investigate? We discover some kind of alien intelligence, and they don't even try to make contact with it? That doesn't make any sense."

"I don't know what the SA did or didn't do. I don't even know if whatever was there was really intelligent in any sense that we could understand. That's beside the point, in any case. The point is, *they didn't want us there*."

He got up from his desk.

"I shouldn't have told you any of this, Lewin. The SA could have my ass if they knew, and the company would probably be glad to offer it up on a plate. Plus, you're too dense even to listen to what I'm saying. So just get out of here, alright?"

"Fishman's World," I said. "That was your last field trip, right?"

"Yes, it was," he said. "And I know what you're thinking. That's where the old guy lost it, right? Well, that's true enough.

"I used to love it—what you do. Jumping around from planet to planet, poking my nose in, solving problems. But you know something? There's nothing that could make me go out there again, ever. The freaking sun could be going supernova and I would sit right here and watch it."

He thumped his desk.

"Get out of here, Lewin," he said again. "And watch your ass."

32

We scrambled out of our flyer and into the largest groundcar available. Theron locked in on the distress signal of the crashed flyer, and we bumped out on the surface of Gehenna.

An hour, more or less. That was how long Theron had thought the trip would take. It was more. The groundcar's progress up and down the hills was excruciatingly slow, the engine often complaining alarmingly. Then we hit a flatter stretch and made steadier progress. But after a few minutes of this we shuddered to a complete halt.

Theron fought with the controls, attempting to put the car into reverse, but with no success.

"We're stuck," she said.

"Stuck?"

"It's probably the ground water. A by-product of the fractionation. You see it sometimes near the main station. Round there it just drains away. But it's rockier here, and the surface soil has become marshy. The tracks are stuck."

"So what are we going to do?"

"What do you think we're going to do? We're going to get out and push."

She got up from the driver's seat.

"Greta," she said, "sit there and wait for my signal. Lewin, you come out with me."

I followed her through the lock and out onto the surface. It was even spookier by night. I could hardly see my hand in front of my face. I took a tentative step after Theron, and immediately my boot sank in the muck up to its ankle.

I froze there for a moment, one foot on the step of the groundcar, one foot in the ground.

We'll sink, I thought. We'll be swallowed alive by this filthy planet.

"Come *on*," Theron said.

Somehow I forced myself to put my other foot into the muck and to shuffle to the front of the car where Theron was already waiting. Theron signalled Vichevski to reverse. We pushed.

It was amusing, in a way, to be reduced to this. Reduced, for all our technology, to this painfully physical labor. Mostly, though, I was afraid. I was never more aware of our appalling vulnerability on this distant and hostile world.

We were a long way from the station, and the station in turn was a very long way from Earth. Suddenly it seemed incredible that I could ever negotiate the return journey. It was just too far, absurdly far, dizzyingly far.

"I don't understand how you do it," Rosemary had said, on more than one occasion. *"How you could go out there."*

The whole trick, I realized now, was in not thinking too closely about what you were doing. Because once you did, sure enough, you were finished. You were no use to anyone, least of all to yourself. That way lay only vertigo, a dreadful vertigo, and, quite possibly, madness.

I had become derailed from my program. I was not sure that I could ever climb back on the tracks.

Later, as I slumped back exhausted in my seat in the car, I was surprised to learn that it had taken a mere twenty minutes of work to free the vehicle. It had seemed like several hours.

"No big deal," Theron said. And in the abstract, of course, I would have had to agree with her. In the abstract.

We drove on, cautiously. We were well into the third hour of our journey from the station when we finally reached the crashed flyer. It lay tilted at a crazy angle, its belly ripped open.

Muller was lying beside the flyer, alive but unconscious, his respiration shallow, his suited arm twisted beneath him. Once we got him into the groundcar and got his suit off we found that his arm was broken. He had also cracked several ribs.

Remus was still strapped into his seat in the flyer. He was dead. The faceplate of his suit was open, as though he had made no effort to close it. But perhaps it had somehow been jarred open by the force of the impact. We dragged his body into the groundcar.

Theron paused to take a vid of the crash site and to remove the log tapes from the control panel of the flyer. Then we began our long and wearisome journey back to Station Gehenna.

I nodded off to sleep. And dreamed, not of Gehenna, but of my childhood on Earth, a quite imaginary childhood. I was playing Little League and my father was watching from the bench, wearing a morose expression.

The expression was right, but the scene was all wrong. I had never played Little League, and if I had my father would never have come to watch me. He had never given me the slightest encouragement to play sports.

I struck out. My father attempted to comfort me in an all-too familiar way.

"Baseball," he said. "What does it matter?"

"It does matter," I said, furious tears welling into my eyes.

And then, miraculously, my father was transformed. He sprouted a long white beard. He reached out to touch my shoulder with his cold metallic hand. I did not flinch.

"You're right, son," he said. "It matters, it all matters, you've got to give a damn, you've got to keep on going. It's a big world out there, it's a big universe. You can do anything you want to do, be anything you want to be, if you have the will to try."

"You can't," I said. "I can't."

"Yes, you can, boy," he said. "Oh yes, you can."

33

Charlotte McKinley appeared oddly calm at the news of her husband's death.

"Poor Norm," she said. "He was such a nice man. Or he was before he got so strange."

I wondered if she would soon say the same thing about me.

"In a strange way," she said, "maybe it's better like this. Norm could never have gone back to living on Earth. The company was his life, it was his whole life."

We placed Remus's body in cold storage for eventual shipment back to Earth, even though McKinley had made a rather bizarre suggestion as to alternative burial arrangements.

"I think we should bury him outside," she said. "Out there. I think he would want that. His body would help the project along, help in the terraforming. That was what he was working for, after all."

"Not really," Theron said. "It wouldn't really make much of a difference."

I doubted very much that Norman Remus would have wanted to be buried here. But in any case, Muller vetoed the suggestion as contrary to the manual of operating procedures.

Muller had regained consciousness on the trip home.

"I don't know what happened," he told us. "Norman was at the controls, but the controls were in any case on automatic. And then he sat forward in his seat, as though he saw something out there, out in the mists. And he muttered something, something that really didn't make much sense. 'No,' he said. 'No. You don't get me.' And then, whether by accident or on purpose, he pushed the manual override. And then we went down like a stone."

"You had time to close your faceplate," Theron said. "Why didn't Remus?"

"Actually, I hadn't opened it yet. We had only just taken off. I guess that Norm had opened his. I don't know why he didn't close it as we went down. It all happened very quickly."

"You said that he seemed to see something," I said. "Did you see anything?"

"What could I see? The moons? I didn't see anything. I really can't account for it."

I believed that I had a fairly good idea of what Remus had seen. I was not quite sure what to do with that information. But I could not keep silent about it any longer.

Wearily I dragged myself back to my quarters and sat down at my terminal. There I wrote, encrypted, and finally transmitted my long overdue report to Sam Haines.

34

Exhausted, I fell into my bed in mid-afternoon, into a deep and dreamless sleep. I was awakened early in the evening by Charlotte McKinley.

Her eyes were bright. She looked less than ever the grieving widow.

"Well?" she asked. "How did she do it?"

"How did who do what?"

"Theron," she said. "How did she make the flyer crash?"

Groggily I climbed out of bed and went into the bathroom to wash my face.

"I think our theory is a bust," I said.

I told her, then, about my brief hallucination in the flyer.

"Whatever that machine is in Theron's laboratory," I said, "it has nothing to do with what I saw, or what Norm must have seen for that matter."

But she was reluctant to concede the point.

"You don't know how it works," she said. "It could have implanted a...what do you call it? A post-hypnotic suggestion."

I considered the idea for a moment.

"I suppose it could have," I said. "Yet it's too neat, and this isn't neat at all. I think there really is something out there."

"That's exactly what she wants you to think. Don't you see that? Because if there is something out there, the company will have to stop this project."

"Maybe I should confront her," I said. "Ask her directly about the machine."

"We've been through that. She'll deny it."

"I've made an interim report to headquarters," I said. "I've outlined the possibility of sabotage here. It's likely they'll send out a security team now. Maybe we should just wait until they come. I'm obviously in over my head here."

"And how long will that take?"

"At least a month."

"In a month," she said, "we may all be dead."

"So what do you suggest? That we go to Muller with what we have?"

"I suggest we wait for R. G. Spooner," she said. "He'll be here the day after tomorrow. He'll know what to do."

"Jesus," I said, suddenly remembering. "We can't let him come here. It's far too dangerous."

"We can dirac and warn him," McKinley said, "then steal a lander and meet his ship."

Her eyes were aglow at the thought of this great adventure. Finally being freed of Norm had apparently cheered her up immensely.

"He would listen to you," McKinley said. "You must have some special code or something that would make him listen."

"You're going too fast," I said. "Let me think about this. Maybe I should just talk to Muller, after all."

"Muller will only defend Theron," she said. "We've been through that too. You've done enough thinking. It's time to *do* something."

She was not altogether wrong. And yet I was less inclined than ever to trust Charlotte McKinley.

35

The next morning I went once again to Valerie Theron's laboratory. She was scanning the log tapes from Muller's flyer. Behind her, the door to the storage cupboard was closed and locked.

"Anything?"

"Nothing."

"Then there's something I must tell you."

I told her, then, of what I had seen on our disastrous sample-gathering expedition, and of what I had seen again in the flyer on our rescue mission. I told her also of my conversations with Remus about his own several visions, and of Remus's beliefs about Arthur Duggan.

She listened quietly, making no comment, raising none of the objections I might have expected. When I had finished she said nothing at all.

"Well?" I asked her. "Do you believe me?"

"Believe what? That you saw what you claim to have seen? I see no reason why you should lie. Believe that what you saw had some reality outside that of your mind? I'm not inclined to believe that."

"But Remus saw it too."

"He claimed to have seen it," she said. "But, alright, let's accept that he did. Psychiatry is hardly my field, but I think the term we're looking for here is *folie à deux*. A shared madness. Somehow Remus infected you with his own obsessions.''

"You're forgetting Arthur Duggan.''

"Make that *à trois*, then, if you like. But we really don't know what Arthur saw.''

"So you see no reason to be concerned about all this?''

"Of course I'm concerned. My husband committed suicide. Another crew member has been killed in a completely unnecessary accident. Still another crew member is being troubled by bizarre hallucinations. Of course I'm concerned. Obviously there is something strange going on at this station. But I can't believe that Arthur Duggan is still, even in some greatly altered form, alive. That's just not possible.''

Here, unexpectedly, she cracked a joke: "It would be a rather interesting question for my lawyers.''

"Duggan is dead enough,'' I said. "I am not claiming that what I saw was in any way real. Obviously it was a delusion. The question is how I was induced to see it, and by whom.''

"You have any ideas on that score?''

"I have several, all rather far-fetched. For example, it could be sabotage. It could be that someone here is trying to destabilize this station and make it impossible for the company to complete this program. An agent of another company perhaps, or more likely, Contractionist elements.''

"Yet how would this saboteur create these delusions?''

"I don't know," I said. "Through some sort of illusion generator or projector, perhaps."

"I have never heard of such a device."

"Technology advances rapidly. It could have been invented only the day before yesterday. After all, we already have dream machines."

"I don't believe they would fit your bill."

"Not as they exist now. But perhaps they could be modified to project more powerfully, and without physical contact with the subject."

She returned my gaze without flinching.

"That's quite a big jump from such a primitive technology to the kind you are proposing."

"Yet a brilliant scientist might make it."

"You are not very subtle, Mr. Lewin," she said. "But I thank you for the compliment all the same. I am not so pleased, though, to learn that you have been spying on me."

"So you admit developing such a machine," I said.

"For my own amusement," she said, "I have been playing around with Vichevski's dream machine, yes. I found the current arrangement primitive, as I said, and I believe I have developed a more sophisticated technique. I am only at the prototype stage right now. But this has nothing to do with your visions. Did I carry this machine onto the flyer?"

"No," I said. "And yet perhaps the delusion, once established, recurs somehow..."

"I am not your saboteur," she said flatly. "Although you can believe what you like."

"I didn't say you were. I was simply putting forward one possible hypothesis. Perhaps it was not an

illusion projector at all. Perhaps it was a hallucino-
genic drug..."

"Perhaps, for that matter, it was food poisoning.
Perhaps it's the chicken salad here. I've always had my
doubts about it. Perhaps McKinley is your saboteur,
whether accidentally or deliberately. In any case, I resent your trying to interrogate me. I'm the one with
the real complaint here, not you. You violated my
privacy, after all. In fact, I really should report your
snooping to Commander Muller. I have nothing to
hide, after all, whereas I believe he would take a dim
view of your own activities."

"Perhaps there is no saboteur," I said. "And yet,
if the problem does not lie inside the station, it must
lie outside. Some alien agency could be at work here."

"That's your other idea?"

I nodded.

"It's certainly far-fetched," she said. "In fact, I
don't know if I would call it an idea at all. It seems to
me more of a fantasy."

"I don't like it very much either. Yet it would fit the
observed facts."

"You have no observed facts, Mr. Lewin. None that
cannot be explained in a more plausible fashion. In
fact, rather than believe in these aliens of yours, I
would much prefer to think that saboteurs are at work.
Not that that's much easier to believe. You know that
all this sounds a bit paranoid? Saboteurs. Delusion
machines. Aliens."

"I know how it sounds," I said. "That is why I need
your help."

"To do what?"

"I want to propose a test."

"To flush out the saboteur?"

"Or the aliens," I said. "Whichever."

"Or neither," she said.

36

Before Theron and I set out on our experiment, I went back to my quarters to check for messages. I was expecting some written response from Haines on my report, very likely a critical one. I was not expecting the communication I did receive.

There was no message from Haines. But almost as soon as I logged on to discover this, a light began to flash to signal a real-time a/v communication. I accepted the call and found myself looking at an executive secretary type.

Was someone calling me from headquarters? The expense would be fantastic. But then, there were elements in my report that might be thought of as fantastic, too.

"One moment," he said. "I have Mr. Spooner on the line."

It was as if he had told me to expect to speak to God. But I hardly had time to panic before I was looking at the florid face of Ronald C. Spooner, Jr.

At least it wasn't the old man, but I was hardly less disconcerted. I realized that he must be communicating with me from his ship, now less than a day from Gehenna. The thought did not make me any happier.

I had seen him in and around the office, of course, but we had never been introduced. Still boyish-looking in his late forties, Ron Jr. was rumored to have a wicked temper, one which grew worse year by year as he waited impatiently to take over the reins of power from his father. I wondered if I was about to feel its sting.

"Lewin," he said. "Haines flashed your report on to me."

"Ah, Mr. Spooner," I said, "we're talking on a clear channel here . . ."

Ron Jr. waved his hand impatiently.

"This is my ship and that's my station," he said, somewhat exaggerating his degree of ownership. "I'll speak to whom I like when I like. And if anyone is listening in, I'll have their ass."

"But the investigation . . ."

"Right, right. I know you've got your methods, and I respect that. Christ knows, you've produced results. But there's no need for any of that cloak-and-dagger bullshit anymore."

"There isn't?"

"Not now that we have your report. I have to congratulate you, Lewin. It's a fine piece of work."

"It is?" I asked, weakly.

"Incisive. To the point. A masterful piece of observation. You can be sure that this contribution will be recognized."

He turned on his smile for me then. It was quite a smile, every molar in plain sight.

If Ron Jr. wanted to snow me, who was I to object? Yet his comments seemed very far out of line

with reality. My investigations here had proved a
shambles, and my report had reflected that. It was a
confused and confusing document. I had expected
Haines to chew me out. I had hardly expected to be
congratulated by the head of my department.

"You understand, sir, that what you have there is
only an interim report..."

"Well, of course. It will need some tightening," he
said. "And you'll have to work up some recommendations. But the hard part is over."

"Recommendations?" I echoed faintly. "I hadn't
exactly reached that stage. As you'll see from my report, there are a number of ways to interpret the situation here, and..."

"Oh, it's very clear to me," he said. "I think it's
very clear."

What was clear? Very little was clear to me.

Sabotage, I thought. He would prefer this to be
sabotage. That way he could keep this project running, once we had rooted out the saboteur. Whereas
if there really was an alien intelligence at work here,
the SA would move in and most likely close us down.

"Well," I said, groping, "I guess sabotage is by far
the simplest explanation..."

The smile froze on Ron Jr.'s face.

"That wasn't what I had in mind."

I was completely confused now. What did this man
want of me?

"You don't think it's sabotage?" I asked.

"No," he said. "I don't. Both Haines and I think
we have strong evidence to support a PAI verdict here.
Of course, you're the man on the spot, and you'll call

it the way you see it. I couldn't ask you to do anything else."

He was grinning at me again, sure of his ground now.

"Haines thinks we have an alien involvement here?"

"Yes, he does," he said. "And Haines is a very experienced man. I've often said how important it was to keep such a man on staff even though there were those who said we should let him go. And now I've been proved right."

After Haines had told me the story of Fishman's World, I had wondered how he had managed to hold on to his job at all. Now I understood. A farsighted manager like Ron Jr. would want to have a man like Haines around. You never knew when you might need him.

"In fact," Ron Jr. continued, "he offered to come out and take a look himself, and you know how Haines feels about going off-planet, but I told him that I was sure it wouldn't be necessary."

"If I conclude alien involvement," I said, "that would be the end of this project. Not necessarily, but probably, given what's already occurred here."

"Like I said, you've got to call it the way you see it," Ron Jr. said. "Better to cut our losses now, than let this drag on any longer, bleeding us white."

"Your father..."

"My father is a businessman," Ron Jr. said. "He'll be able to read the score, don't you worry about that."

"And yet," I said, "I've been unable to rule out entirely the possibility of sabotage. Perhaps you should send in a security team..."

He got angry then.

"Don't tell me who I should send in," he shouted, his face becoming redder still. "Just write your report. I'll expect personal delivery of it tomorrow, when we come down to that rathole of a station."

"Under the circumstances," I said, "I'm not sure it would be advisable for you or your father to—"

"And don't tell me what's advisable," he said, his anger out of control now. "We're coming down, that's all. No way I'm going to miss this, no way in the world.

"My father drags me halfway across the galaxy like I was still some five-year-old salivating for a candy bar. 'You've got to see it, Ronnie,' he says. 'See what it's really like out there. See it before you're ready to run it—you always did take after your mother, running and hiding behind her skirts. You gotta see what this is about and then maybe, just maybe, I'm going to step down the way I've been promising you these past ten, fifteen years....'"

He stopped and made a deliberate effort to calm himself.

"You're a psychologist, Lewin. What the hell, I don't have to spell it out for you. You know about this father-son stuff. Not that it has anything to do with my mother, you understand. It's between me and the old man—we never did get along so well, and lately it's been getting worse.

"I never wanted to work for the company, you know. I wanted to be a farmer, that was what I wanted when I was a kid. But he pleaded with me, told me there had to be a Spooner in here and it had to be me. Well, he's kept me waiting a long time now, to run this company, and all the time he's been running it into the ground. This is just his latest screw-up, although it's a beauty."

"I understand," I said. "And yet it could still be dangerous for you..."

"What I'm saying is, this is important to me. You can bet I'm not going to pass up this chance to show him what's happened to this crazy little project of his. You can bet on it.

"You're an intelligent man, Haines tells me. A bit of a jerk, but an intelligent man. I think you understand what's at stake here. I think you understand that I can do you a lot of good, particularly after tomorrow. Don't be a jerk, Lewin. Don't screw me around. I'll see you tomorrow."

He cut the connection.

I sat staring at the empty screen.

He's coming down here, I thought. He wants me to report that there are dangerous alien life forms here, and yet he's coming down. No matter how badly he wants to show up his father, would he really do that if he actually believed in those aliens? Surely not. He did not strike me as a reckless man.

But if he didn't believe in aliens, what did he believe was going on here? If we ruled out mass delusion, and I had effectively ruled it out in my report, the only remaining possibility was sabotage. And yet, if he believed it was sabotage, why would he deliberately expose himself and his father to the danger presented by this saboteur?

He might do so if he believed himself in some way safe from that saboteur. If he himself were the man pulling the strings, the man controlling that saboteur. If, that is, he had been working all along for the failure of this project and the downfall of his father.

It was not a very comforting explanation, but I was unable to think of a better one.

"You're the man on the spot," he had told me. *"You'll call it the way you see it."*

The irony was that I had been increasingly inclined to believe that there were aliens at work here. To believe, that is, precisely what Ron Jr. wished me to believe, what he may well have orchestrated events to lead me to believe. Now he had given me good reason to doubt that premise.

If I was right, then I had been manipulated toward that conclusion from the very beginning, at first subtly and now quite directly.

Would I go along with Ron Jr.'s desires? Would I, as Rosemary might have put it, embrace my situational unfreedom and go with the flow? Or would I, as Ron Jr. had put it, decide to be a jerk?

I thought of teaching intro psych and cleaning rat cages. I thought about being a permie, swilling beer and watching the screen. I thought about Earth. It could only be an improvement on places like this.

And yet, even if I decided to call it the way I really saw it, how did I see it? For the moment, I was suffering from double vision at the very least. I could only hope that my forthcoming expedition with Valerie Theron would help clear my sight.

37

"I propose," I had told Valerie Theron, "to attempt to make contact with this supposed lifeform, whatever it is. I would like your assistance."

Of course, as Theron herself must have realized, I had a hidden agenda here. If there was indeed a saboteur among us, then my primary candidate was Theron herself.

It was not only the business of the dream projector, although that was troublesome enough. There was also the curious failure of my suit radio on our first expedition outside to consider. And it seemed to me that she had been less forthcoming in her testimony concerning the mental state of Arthur Duggan.

And yet if I was right, I could be exposing myself to considerable risk. If Theron was indeed responsible for the deaths of Duggan and Remus, she might well be prepared to kill again. Perhaps that was why she had consented to accompany me on this voyage of discovery.

Even if I were to successfully expose her as the saboteur and make a safe return to the station, my career would surely be in ruins, for the anger of Ron Jr. would be fearful to see. Unless I could somehow connect Theron to him, and bring them both down . . .

On the whole, I was almost hoping for contact with aliens, much as that prospect terrified me.

"This is rather above the call of duty for a leisure officer," Theron said, as our groundcar left the station behind.

"I have a personal stake in this."

"And a professional one."

"I'm sorry?"

"You're some sort of detective, aren't you? We suspected as much from the beginning."

"We?"

"The crew. Even before you arrived, we figured there would have to be an investigation of Duggan's death, one way or another. And when you showed up, you seemed to be the obvious candidate."

"I'm not a detective," I said, a little wearily.

"But something like it."

"Yes," I said. "Something like it."

I told her then. At this point it didn't seem to make much difference. Tomorrow everyone would know. Tomorrow, one way or another, my work here would be at an end.

We moved on toward our test location, the spot where we had gathered samples only a few days ago, where I had first seen the giant figure of Arthur Duggan.

"There's something else strange," I said, suddenly struck by an insight. "It didn't occur to me before, but there may be a kind of pattern to all this. For some reason, these visions have only affected the men. First Duggan, apparently, then Remus, then me. All of us except Muller, who probably wouldn't tell us even if he had experienced the same thing."

"Yes?" Theron asked. "What's your point? You're suggesting that we're dealing with a cabal of feminist saboteurs? Or feminist aliens? You think we're all out to get you?"

The Contractionists, as I now recalled, had been strongly influenced by old-time feminism, and their leadership was indeed primarily female. But that was not what I had been getting at.

"I'm just suggesting that men are more susceptible. Or perhaps just more guilty."

"Guilty? Guilty of what?"

"It could be argued," I said, "that what we're doing here on Gehenna could be characterized as a distinctly male enterprise. The outcome, if you like, of eons of sociobiological programming to dominate and destroy our environment. So in that sense men may be more culpable here. Vichevski suggested as much to me a few days ago."

"Isn't it a little late in the day for consciousness raising?" Theron asked. "In any case, I don't think I like that line of thought. It suggests that I am merely an appendage to the process going on here, where in fact I must share full responsibility for it."

"But in a philosophical sense..."

"In a philosophical sense, perhaps," she said. "But unless we're dealing here with philosophical aliens..."

She did not complete the thought. The groundcar had come to its programmed halt. We closed the face-plates of our suits. Theron took a five-meter length of cable and attached it to her belt, then to my own, linking us like Siamese twins. Or perhaps, I thought, mother and child.

She picked up a vidcamera and handed it to me. She strapped a combination radio receiver/tape machine over her shoulder.

"Well," she said, "I feel very foolish about this now, and I will feel even more foolish afterward. But let's do it."

We clambered out of the car and took up a position as close as we could reconstruct to where I had stood a few days before. The beep of the car's homing signal sounded reassuringly in my ears.

We stood watching and waiting. The mists swirled around as usual, surrounding us in a bare, dead-white blankness. Nothing happened.

"Alright," Theron said, finally. "Try switching off your radio."

"Why?"

"To approximate conditions the other day. Maybe you need to be out of contact, to be a little panicky. Switch it off and try to concentrate on contacting...whatever it is you think may be out there. If you do see something, run the camera. I'm going to turn off my radio, too. Just tug on the cable when you want to resume contact."

"OK," I said, although I did not much like the idea.

We stood in silence for a few minutes. The murk was so thick I could hardly make out the outlines of Theron's suit. The groundcar was quite invisible. I felt very alone and cut off. Would Theron try to kill me now? Would I see the giant Duggan again, or something even more terrifying? Predictably, the panic began to well up.

I wondered now what I hoped to prove by all this. Suppose I did see something? It could be just another post-hypnotic suggestion, another programmed delusion. Or suppose Theron did attack me? Out here, on terrain far more familiar to her than to me, she would be at a definite advantage.

It was almost as if I was deliberately fuelling my own anxiety. As if I knew that whatever was out there would only respond to me in that state.

And then the scream resounded inside my head. It bypassed my ears completely; it had nothing whatsoever to do with radio signals. The scream was both human and inhuman, anguished and exultant. It spoke of terrible pleasure and of terrible pain. It was nearly overpowering.

And then the murk thinned out to a wispy mist, thinned out for klicks around, so that I could see the groundcar quite clearly, see Theron jerking her head back in amazement to gaze at the spectacular sight of the blazing white sun of Gehenna visible in the heavens. The moss beneath my feet began to shrivel and turn black under the glare. It was as if, quite suddenly, our work on this planet was complete, as if we had already succeeded in our transformation of the biosphere.

Then I saw the giants looming over us. First Arthur Duggan, by now a familiar figure, his outline becoming less distinct with each passing moment, smiling vaguely as his very substance seemed to boil away under that remorseless sun.

"Goodbye, Arthur," I think I may have said. "They're all finished with you now."

For what it was worth, I triggered the camera.

As Duggan ebbed away, a new figure took his place. This one was much sharper, clearer-edged, and it seemed to glow with reflected energy. This one was a woman. She was no woman I had ever seen before, and every woman. She was huge, naked, splendid. She was screaming, and I realized that it was her scream I had been hearing all along.

The scream was changing pitch now, becoming softer, almost crooning. As it swept over me I felt a sexual desire that was at once almost painfully intense and strangely undifferentiated. It was desire for her, perhaps, that hopelessly unattainable giant who towered above me, yet it was also desire for Theron, for McKinley, for every woman.

She wanted me.

Let yourself go, I told myself, as Rosemary might have told me. Give up control. Give up your boundaries. Merge yourself with the infinite.

And yet I could not.

Rather than merge myself with this wondrous vision, I attempted only to contact it, following the program I had agreed with Theron.

Tell me, I signalled urgently. Tell me what you want of me. Of us.

But she had no words for me, no explanations. Only that crooning scream.

Desperate to make sense of this giant woman, I began to stumble toward her, unwittingly dragging

Theron along behind me. I had taken four or five paces when the mists closed down around me as suddenly as they had lifted. Then it was Theron's turn to tug me back toward the groundcar.

38

"Remarkable," Theron said, as she flipped open her faceplate. "I've never seen a fluctuation like that. To see the sun itself."

"The sun? Was that all you saw? You didn't see her?"

"Her?"

"You didn't hear her?"

"I heard . . . something," Theron said, with apparent reluctance. "Inside my head, somehow. A sort of tugging sensation. I thought it was just my imagination. It was sort of . . ."

"Sexy," I completed.

"Yes," she agreed. "Isn't that strange?"

I had a sudden vision, then, of the two of us tearing off our atmosphere suits, then our inner clothing, to make love on the hard plasticated floor of the groundcar.

I do not know whether anything similar ran through her mind.

We drove back to the station in silence, thinking our own private thoughts.

The vidfilm, predictably, showed nothing: nothing, that is, beyond the startling atmospheric shift that revealed the sun of Gehenna. The audio tapes were quite blank.

"Unfortunately," Theron said, "you seem to be no further advanced. Whatever you may think you experienced out there, you have no objective evidence to support it. You have proved neither sabotage nor the presence of aliens."

No doubt she would have wanted to submit the matter to a properly controlled experiment to be analyzed using the proper nonparametric statistical method. Once upon a time I might have agreed with her.

"I know what I believe," I said. "I know what I must recommend. But for the moment it doesn't really matter. Aliens or saboteurs, we cannot allow the Spooners to land here."

I would give Ron Jr. the report he wanted, I thought. But not in person. And if that was unsatisfactory to him, then very soon I would no longer be employed by his company. But if that was how it would have to go down, that was how it would go down.

39

"You must deny R. G. Spooner permission to land here," I told Muller. "You must do this for his own safety. It's within your authority: I've looked it up."

"On what grounds?" Muller asked, astonished.

"I believe that there is sentient life here, life which is hostile, or at least dangerous toward us. At the same time, there is some reason to believe that we may have a saboteur among us. Either reason should be sufficient for you to deny this landing."

"Sentient life? Saboteurs? What nonsense is this?" Muller listened to my account in growing agitation.

"In fact," I concluded, "I believe that you should shut down the terraforming machinery right now, to avoid any further damage to the native lifeforms and to avoid provoking further hostility directed toward us."

"Shut down the machines?" Muller echoed. "Deny landing permission to the chairman? All this simply on your say-so? I know this has been a very stressful experience for you here, Lewin, but I did not realize how badly it had affected you. Surely you don't expect me to listen to this foolishness? I cannot accept it, any of it, not for a single moment. As for you, I believe that

I must relieve you of your duties and request your immediate recall.''

"By all means," I said. "Relieve me of my duties as leisure officer. Because I am not a leisure officer. I am a psychologist in the investigative field services group for R. G. Spooner. As such I have the authority, in an emergency situation, to take command of this station if necessary. Let me give you formal notice that I regard this as an emergency situation and will not hesitate to take the appropriate steps."

"You have identification to support this claim?"

"Of course I don't have identification," I said, irritated. "I'm working undercover here, I'm hardly going to carry around something advertising that fact. You can check with headquarters easily enough."

Muller looked, uncertainly, to Theron, who had remained silent throughout my presentation.

"Is this true?"

"Is what true?"

"That he is a company investigator?"

"So he has claimed to me. It seems likely. It would explain his otherwise peculiar behavior here."

"And what of his theories?" Muller asked. "Do you believe in this nonsense about a living biosphere?"

"It's a rather incredible hypothesis, obviously, and I am reluctant to accept it without better evidence. I cannot personally confirm his own account of our test out there. As your science officer, I don't think I can make any recommendation at all.

"And yet, speaking personally, I believe he may be right in suggesting that it would be dangerous for the chairman to visit here. Given our recent events, perhaps that visit should be postponed, at least until we have a fuller understanding of the situation."

"I understand the situation well enough," Muller said. "I understand that this man has cracked. I understand that I have been given an impossible team to work with here from the beginning. First Duggan, then Norm, now him. Unstable, every one of them. That's what I understand."

"Something is making your people crack, Commander Muller," I told him. "That's what I've been trying to tell you. I suggest that you send the message denying landing permission, right now. Or else I must assume control here and send it myself."

"Oh yes?" Muller asked. "And how do you propose to do that?"

"How would you stop me?" I asked. "You have a broken arm, after all."

"Even with a broken arm, I believe you would present me with little difficulty. But if we are going to exchange threats, let me point out that I also have a weapon."

He opened his desk drawer and pulled out a laser pistol, which he levelled at me.

"Just as important," he said, "I believe that I can count on the loyalty of the station's crew."

He looked at Theron. She made no comment for or against this statement.

"Investigator or not," he told me, "you are acting in a decidedly unbalanced manner. I must ask you to remain in your quarters until I can dirac Earth to straighten out this question of your identity. If you are indeed who you claim to be, I will forward your recommendations to the appropriate parties who will take them under consideration. In the meantime, the work continues, and we look forward to a visit from the chairman."

He stood up, still holding the laser pistol trained at me.

"After you," he said.

40

The door to my quarters was sealed and programmed on the station computer to remain so. I was effectively imprisoned.

I was not yet much concerned about my situation. Once Muller received confirmation of my identity, he would have to let me out of here. And then, even if he would not agree to deny landing permission to the Spooners, he would at least have to pass on my warning. Of course, Ron Jr. might still try to keep that information from his father, yet perhaps I could contact the old man directly.

The waiting, however, quickly began to get on my nerves. It seemed to me that they were taking a very long time over a simple piece of business.

The door to my quarters did not open again until 2000 hours, when McKinley brought me a tray of food from the cafeteria, triggering the door release from the outside. I cheered up at this sight of a potential ally. Theron had let me down, but McKinley might yet come through for me.

McKinley seemed oddly jumpy. She placed the tray on the floor without a word, and backed away toward the door.

"Don't you want to hear the latest on my investigations?" I asked. "There have been some interesting developments."

"No," she said. "Because you're not a detective, not even a psychologist. In fact, we think you must be the saboteur here."

"That's crazy," I said. "The dirac from Earth will tell you just how crazy. I'm surprised they haven't received it yet."

"It's been received, alright. It has confirmed you as no more or less than a leisure officer."

"There's been some mix-up," I said, stunned. "Some mistake."

"No mistake. I saw the printout myself. Theron brought it to Muller in the cafeteria."

"Theron..." I said. "Then it was Theron, all along. She was the saboteur, just as you said. And now she's faked the dirac. For some reason, she wants the old man to land here. Perhaps she's planning to take a shot at him."

I got up from my chair.

"You have to help me," I said. "We've got to stop this. Spooner will be here first thing tomorrow."

"Not another step," she said, bringing up a laser pistol from the pocket of her tunic.

"Theron is lying," I said. "I am what I claim to be."

"I don't think you know what you are. I think you've come to believe your own lies."

"It doesn't matter whether you believe me or not. I must speak to Muller. I've got to get out of here."

"You're going to stay right there," she said, aiming the pistol at me and backing out of the door.

"Then tell Muller to come here. Or at least tell Muller to check. Tell him to call Ron Jr. on the ship. He knows who I am. He'll identify me..."

As if in answer, the door whirred shut in my face.

I crossed to my terminal to punch in Muller's code. The terminal was dead.

I lay down on my bed and stared at the ceiling. For a moment I played with the idea that McKinley had advanced, that I was no more or less than a leisure officer. Perhaps my own conviction that I was a psychologist was just one more delusion, like my vision of the goddess who waited for me in the mists. It would make my life a good deal easier if that were so. I would have no further responsibility for unraveling this puzzle here, no need to concern myself about the fate of R. G. Spooner and son.

I almost wished that it was true.

41

Somehow I was lulled by boredom into an uneasy sleep. I woke hours later, stretched out fully clothed on my bed, to find the door of my quarters open. There was no one in the corridor outside. The quiet was almost eerie.

As I sat up I realized that what I was hearing was complete silence. The familiar hum of the terraforming equipment was absent.

Had Muller taken my advice after all and shut down his machines? But if he had, then why had he not come to release me as well?

I hesitated at the doorway for a moment, as if uncertain of where I was going. And then, with growing conviction, I walked through the empty corridors toward the central control room.

It was midway through the sleep cycle and there was no sign of life of any sort. But the fluorescent lights still burned at full luminescence, turning the high-gloss green paint of the walls into a mirror reflecting my own bloated and distorted face.

The control room was a shambles. The banks of machinery controlling the terraforming process had been wrecked beyond repair. The indicators from the substations were dead. The dirac equipment had been destroyed, too. I could not even attempt to warn off Spooner's ship,

The control room was empty. But there was blood on the floor, a thin trail of blood. I followed it out the door and down a corridor. At the end of this trail I found Muller slumped at the door of his living quarters. It was amazing that he had been able to get even this far. Half his skull had been caved in, as though by a blow from a heavy instrument. He was quite dead, and already cool to the touch.

I stepped past Muller's body and triggered the door to his quarters. Vichevski was asleep in their bed, breathing steadily. I left her sleeping and stepped out again, closing the door behind me.

I checked the wall intercom in the corridor. The station's internal communications network, at least, was still working. I called McKinley.

"This is Lewin," I said. "Listen to me carefully now. Theron has run amok. She killed Muller and wrecked the control room. Muller's body is in the corridor just outside his living quarters. Come here and take care of Vichevski. I'm going to find Theron."

"You killed Muller," McKinley told me. "And now you're waiting there to kill me. But I'm not going to come. And if you come here, remember, I still have a pistol."

"Theron did it," I said. "Then she opened the door of my quarters to implicate me. In any case, I don't have time to argue about this. Just do what I said."

42

I cut the connection and set off in search of Theron. Where would she be? Maybe in the vehicle bay, waiting to get a shot at Spooner. I set off toward the main airlock.

There was blood on the sleeve of my jacket. Muller's blood. I paused to try to wipe it off, but succeeded only in spreading it on to my hands. Then I tried to wipe my hands on my trousers.

Macbeth, I thought. Except that he was guilty and I'm not.

I suppressed a giggle. Plainly, I was on the edge of hysteria.

I realized that I had become disoriented. I had arrived not at the main airlock but at Airlock Two. I found myself staring out the very same observation portal through which I had seen Norman Remus communing with the mysteries of Gehenna, and where Remus, in turn, had seen Arthur Duggan.

Outside the station, the murk that was the atmosphere of Gehenna seemed almost tranquil. And yet the voices that were suddenly inside my head were more powerful than ever, more agonized and more passionate.

I found myself, with no memory of the transition, at the door of Airlock Two. I punched the button and the door rolled open in front of me. I stepped through and punched another button to close it.

The row of empty atmosphere suits stared down at me from the wall, but I walked past them unhesitatingly to the opposite door, the one which led out to the surface of Gehenna. I punched in the code for the door to open. It did not.

I paused, confused, as the safety program cut in.

"Exit denied," said the autovoice. *"Sensors indicate that you are inadequately protected."*

"Override," I said dreamily.

"Regulations do not permit exit without adequate protection for ground conditions," the door told me.

"Override," I said again.

"Regulations . . ." the program began again. It was not a very sophisticated program.

"I heard you," I said.

I pulled down a suit from the wall and began to pull it on. It was then that it hit me, the answer to the puzzle that Norman Remus had originally posed me.

"Clue," I said, as the pieces, suddenly, fell into place. It was clear to me, finally, that Arthur Duggan had been murdered. Or at least, assisted in his own suicide. I also knew how it had been done.

The safety program had not failed, and neither could Duggan himself have been in any state of mind at the end to try to fool it. Instead, he must have had an accomplice in his own undoing. Someone at the board of the main computer had temporarily overridden this circuit to permit his exit. That someone, I realized now, was Duggan's own wife, Valerie Theron.

I knew all this with a part of my mind, and yet somehow I did not care at all, except to wish that someone would perform the same service for me.

I watched, in a detached way, as my fingers again punched the exit mechanism. Again the door refused to open.

Sensors indicate that faceplate remains unsealed.

I flipped the plate into place. And at last the door rolled open. At last I stepped out onto the surface. At last I was ready to let go, to merge, to become everything and nothing at once, to dissolve myself utterly.

The voices in my head reached a triumphant crescendo, as Gehenna sang out its welcome.

It would have been nice to go out like Arthur Duggan, to roll naked in the glorious moss, to wrap myself in its whiteness. But I was encumbered by that clumsy atmosphere suit. At least I could breathe Gehenna's sweet, sweet air.

I reached up to open my faceplate. And then a gloved hand grabbed my arm. A helmeted face loomed toward me out of the mist. I could not make out the features. McKinley, I thought, in an abstracted way. Come out to try and save me.

"Lewin," said the voice in my headphones. "For chrissakes snap out of it. What are you trying to do?"

We struggled. The other figure was strong, but I was stronger, my desire to taste the sweetness of Gehenna overpowering. I threw the other to the ground.

"Don't try to stop me, Charlotte," I said, as she rose to a crouch. "This is right, you must see that. She wants me..."

"This is Valerie Theron," the other said, standing up, walking toward me so I could see that it was true.

I hesitated. Something was puzzling me, nagging at the rational, reasoning part of my mind....

"I don't get it," I said. "Why try to stop me? I'm finishing the job for you, after all, so it's all working out for the best. I only wish you had made things easier for me, the way you did for Duggan. You could have overridden the safety program so I didn't have to bother with this suit."

"That's right," she said. "Why try to stop you? Think it through, Lewin. Apply your wonderful powers of deduction."

Even as poor a detective as I had proved to be could now make the final selection from my rather diminished pool of suspects.

"McKinley," I said. "It was McKinley."

I had seen McKinley's skills as a programmer already. It was McKinley who must have sped Arthur Duggan on his way by cancelling the safety program; McKinley who had tried to divert suspicion to Theron; McKinley who had tried to confuse me for the last time that very night.

"She lied to me about the dirac," I said. "She killed Muller and she wrecked the machines. She unlocked my door to set me up to take the blame."

The voices were dimming now in my head, dying out. The impulse to open my faceplate was still present, but no longer overpowering.

"Let's go back inside."

As we emerged through the inner door into the station, we saw a tall man with a long white beard and metal hand standing there, as if waiting for us.

"What the hell" he said, "is going on here?"

43

Just behind R. G. Spooner stood his son, looking red-faced and angry. And behind them, two armed men, obviously their personal bodyguards.

"We got here a little early," Spooner said. "Couldn't raise you on the radio so we came down to find out why not, and it looks like it's just as well. We just came from the control room. Some fun." He made this pronouncement with a certain relish.

Ron Jr. stepped forward as I struggled out of my suit.

"This man," he said, indicating me, "works for me. If you'll allow me to question him..."

"He works for me, too," his father reminded him. "You all work for me, come to think of it. Last I heard, anyway."

He was staring with frank interest at the blood on my jacket.

"Some party," he said.

"Lewin," Ron Jr. asked, "what in God's name has been happening here?"

"More of the same," I said. I felt a little dizzy. "Aliens and saboteurs. Attempted suicide and successful murder. More of the same."

"Murder?"

"Franz Muller," I said. "He's dead. And this time, murder is the only thing it could have been." I waved my hand in the direction of his quarters.

Ron Jr. seemed shaken by this news, but he recovered himself quickly enough. He turned to his father.

"You see," he said. "This is even worse than we thought. The repercussions.... We've no choice but to pull out now, shut it all down and get out of here."

"No choice?" Spooner echoed. "Is that what you think?"

"I've always told you this project was a bad mistake. I hope you can see that now."

But his father waved him away, as if swatting at some irksome insect.

"We've got plenty of choices," he said. "Lots of them."

"You shouldn't have come down here at all," I told him. "I tried to get Muller to warn you."

"You wanted to warn me off?" Spooner laughed. "That would have only guaranteed that I come take a look for myself. Alright, let's hear it. Tell me what's been happening here."

"There's a killer in this station," I said. "I think we should take care of her first."

"Alright," Spooner said. "Agreed. We can't have a killer running around loose. But how do I know it wasn't you? Or her." He nodded toward Theron.

"You don't know that. For the moment you'll have to take my word for it. Like your son told you, I work for him, indirectly. My name is Victor Lewin, and I'm a psychological investigator."

"Like that son of a bitch Sam Haines," Spooner said. "Never did have much time for you people, but we won't get into that now. What about her?"

He indicated Theron.

"She just saved my life."

"Saved it from what?"

"From Gehenna," I said.

"What nonsense are you talking, Lewin?" Ron Jr. asked, but again Spooner waved him aside. Other than a slight furrowing of his forehead he seemed not to react to my statement.

"Alright," Spooner said, "let's go get your killer. But we'll keep you all under guard for the moment." He motioned to his bodyguards. "Who are we looking for?"

"Charlotte McKinley," I said.

"The food lady. Is that right?" Spooner cackled in secret amusement. He turned to his son. "Looks like your game here has run a little out of control."

"I don't know what you mean," Ron Jr. said. "What are you talking about?"

"Don't try to lie to me, Ronnie—you never could and in this case you shouldn't even try. I know all about it. You see, I still know almost everything that happens in this company, even now. I got people who are loyal to me, even in your own office. People a lot more loyal than my own son. So I knew you had this McKinley woman on your payroll, although for a while I couldn't figure out why. She was your eyes and ears here, and apparently quite a bit more."

"She wasn't supposed..."

"Save it," Spooner said. "We'll discuss it later, you bet we will. But right now we got to take care of her first. Lead on, Levine."

"Lewin," I said.

Spooner walked as briskly as any of us as I led the way to Muller's quarters. We found his body still in the same place.

"Messy," Spooner said cheerfully. He was obviously enjoying himself enormously.

Inside the room, Vichevski was crying and McKinley was trying to comfort her. Theron and I came through the door first. McKinley seemed shocked to see us together.

"I thought he'd killed you," she told Theron. "The way he killed Muller."

"You killed Muller," Theron said. "And Arthur Duggan, too. I don't know about Norm Remus. Maybe you arranged that as well."

"I didn't kill Arthur," she said. "I just helped him do what he wanted to do. And what she wanted him to do. She wanted him so badly."

"She?" Theron asked.

"Gehenna," said R. G. Spooner from the doorway. He came into the room. "She means the planet itself, or something close to it. Some kind of meta-organization of life forms here."

"You don't seem very surprised," I said.

Spooner laughed aloud. "I discovered this planet, sonny, before you were even born. Left a piece of myself here, for that matter. You're telling me I should be surprised?"

"You're telling us that you ordered this planet terraformed knowing there was sentient life here?"

"Exactly," said that crazy old man. "That's exactly what I'm telling you."

I looked around the room. Even Ron Jr. seemed stunned by the enormity of this statement.

"There really are aliens here?" he asked. "I thought, I thought . . ."

"You thought you'd take the company away from me, that's what you thought. Invent a few aliens and wheel out your nervous nellie Sam Haines and bring in the SA. Write off our investment here, watch our shares take a dive, and knock daddy off at the next annual meeting, if he wouldn't go quietly first. I know what you thought. Aliens here? Well, of course there are. And what difference does that make?

"Settle down, kiddies," he said. "I've got a story to tell you."

44

"We were tired," Spooner told us. "More tired than you could imagine. Even I was tired. And we'd already found enough new worlds to keep mankind busy for a hundred years."

"Humanity," Theron said. "I think you mean humanity."

"Whatever. We'd found what we were looking for. New worlds, green worlds, empty worlds, ready for the taking. Wealth, sitting there in the ground for us, ready to be dug up.

"If I was a gambling man I would say that we were on a roll, we just couldn't help but win. We hit the jackpot every time we pulled the handle. Although for me it was more like fishing. Every time we threw the hook in the water there was another big one ready to bite.

"It's hard to stop yourself when everything is going your way. Even when you're exhausted. Even when you want to get home and climb into your own bed. Even when the night is coming down and the wind is coming up. As long as the fish are biting, it's hard to stop.

"One more, I kept telling my crew. Just one more. It was greedy, I suppose, yet it seemed almost like fate, that we were fated to be doing this. And so we pushed ourselves onward, on and on. On to Gehenna.

"We made our survey from orbit, and we found indications of significant mineral deposits. But all in all, it wasn't terribly promising, what with the heat and the atmosphere. Forget it, that was what my crew told me, forget about staking a claim. We can't even land here, and even if we could, what would be the point? No one is ever gonna want to develop this planet. This ain't no fish, this is just some rotten old boot, throw it back and wind up your line. Forget it, just forget it, we're tired and we wanna go home, we've seen quite enough of this big old universe already.

"And yet I couldn't help but think that I had come here for a purpose, the way I had found all those other worlds for a purpose. I couldn't believe that purpose was just to turn tail and run home.

"It was white, then, you know, this planet. Awfully white. I would look down upon it for hours at a time, I just couldn't tear my eyes away, As white as a snowball, as white as a cloud, as white as the foam on the waves, as white as an old-time wedding gown. Dead white, as far as the eye could see, bare white, a terrible whiteness, it hurt your eyes just to look at it but you couldn't keep yourself from looking.

"It was hateful, in a way, all that blankness, it was like you could just empty out your mind into it, lose yourself in it. There were no limits, there were no boundaries; you would have to keep on reminding yourself who you were. But like I said, it was fascinating, too.

"So I pulled out all the data on our equipment, checked out all the safety limits. I figured out that yes, if we were careful, and maybe just a little bit lucky, we could go down and take a closer look at that pale lady. Go down there without getting fried to a crisp; long enough to poke around a little and stake our claim, anyway.

"My crew didn't really want to hear that. But I told them, you got to think of the future. Right now it looks like there are planets for the plucking everywhere. But we're not the only company doing this, and right now we're about as far out as anyone would want to go for another hundred years. One day this is gonna look like a nice piece of real estate.

"Oh, sure, it was hot. But we could take care of that, stir up a little dust, deflect the solar radiation for awhile, cool it down nicely. That was what they were going to do to Venus, you know, when I was a boy: nuke the hell out of Venus. That was back before we got the space drive, when there seemed some reason to want to go live on Venus. And Venus was a helluva lot hotter.

"And, sure, the air was poison. But we could do something about that, too. There was no reason to let this planet beat us, no reason at all.

"Everything I said made sense. I could be pretty persuasive, you know, back then. I think I even persuaded myself. They still didn't like it, but enough of them went along. I'd made them rich men already, every one of them. They *owed* it to me. I took four men down with me, down to that burning hot snow-ball.

"And for awhile everything went well. We got some fabulous assays. The equipment held up fine. And then..."

He broke off to stare contemplatively at his mechanical hand, as if unsure how to continue.

"You had an accident," I said. "A crewman's life was in danger, and you saved him but you lost your hand."

R. G. Spooner laughed. He laughed so hard that tears came to his eyes and spittle to his lips.

"You must have been reading my bio," he said finally, his shoulders still shaking with mirth. "That public affairs boy did a helluva job. Oh, what a lovely bunch of bullshit. Fact is, one of my crew saved me. You see, I took off my glove."

"You what?" Ron Jr. said. "Mother said..."

"I never could have explained it to your mother," the old man said. "Could hardly explain it to myself, afterward. We were sleeping in the shelter, it was our last night on Gehenna. In the morning we were going to pack up our gear and head back to the ship. I'm not sure if I'd already named it Gehenna, I think that must have been later, as I remember I was leaning to Snowball or something like that.

"In any case, I was sleeping. And I had the strangest dream. I guess you might call it a sex dream, although it wasn't like any sex dream I'd ever had before, and in any case I hadn't had any dreams like that since I was a kid. It wasn't that I was sexually frustrated, you understand. It's true that I hadn't seen my wife in two years but she was never much in that department and we had women in the crew in any case, not that I'm proud of that . . ."

"Dad," Ron Jr. said. "I don't know if I want to hear this stuff."

"Well, alright, Ronnie, alright. I was just trying to put this thing in context a little. In any case, if you don't want to hear that, you won't like what comes next, either. You see, in my dream it was like I heard voices calling to me, calling me out of the shelter. And in my dream I got up from by bed, bare-ass naked, and I walked to the lock, and I walked right through it, into the whiteness. Walked out on the moss, soft as a carpet, and it didn't burn my feet at all, didn't even tickle. And I took a deep breath, a wonderful deep breath. And then I saw her, waiting for me.

"How could I describe her to you? I couldn't describe her. No offense to your mother, Ronnie, but she was the woman I'd been looking for all my life, the woman every man looks for."

"Some sort of archetype," Theron said. "Drawn directly from your subconscious."

"Whatever," Spooner said.

"A giant?" I asked. "A giant woman?"

"Yes, she was. She was. And yet somehow that didn't matter, not when we lay down on that moss together and made love, she wasn't a giant anymore or maybe she was—I don't know, maybe it was me who got bigger. But in any case I've had a lot of women, before and since, hundreds I guess, but this wasn't like it had been with any one of them. It was like fucking the whole universe, you know, sinking down into the void, being absorbed, giving myself up completely somehow, so that there was no me in there at all. Of course by this point I was close to being dead, and yet in a way, I've got to tell you, it felt terrific.''

"You were walking in your sleep," Theron said.

"Yes, I was. Never did it before, never did it again, once was quite enough. I was sleeping in my atmosphere suit, fortunately, not naked like in the dream. We all were, otherwise I wouldn't be telling you this now. I got up and walked across the room to the lock. One of my crew members saw me, couldn't figure what the hell I was doing. By the time he'd decided to follow I was already outside. He found me out there, humping the moss. Must have been quite a sight to see. I'd managed to pull off one glove, I was digging with my bare hand in the moss. The flesh was melting away.

"They had to amputate it, of course."

He flexed his mechanical limb.

"Never mind, though," he said. "Never mind. Accidents will happen. Don't look back. In the end you've got to keep on going.

"I never told anyone about this before," he said. "Just told my crew I was under a lot of stress, I must have blown a fuse, it was time to go home. More or less convinced myself of the same thing, although I guess I knew, deep down, knew it really happened, happened just the way I dreamed it. I thought about seeing a shrink, but I never had much time for that sort of thing. So I never told anyone, until now. I've hardly even thought about it in years.

"Gehenna. I put it down on the claim as Gehenna. Good name, don't you think?"

"Hell of a name," I said.

"You sent us here," Vichevski said, face contorted with anger, "knowing all this?"

"Well, yes and no. I thought she was dead, you see, if she was ever here to begin with. That was what I told myself, anyway. I thought the nukes would have finished her off for sure. I never thought..."

For a moment I thought he might actually be about to apologize, but he stopped himself.

"This is a risky business," he told her. "Even now. You all know the risks, that's why we pay you as well as we do."

"My husband is dead," Vichevski told him. "And this planet killed him, one way or another."

"I'm sorry about your husband, of course. But he always knew something like this could happen."

"No, he didn't," Vichevski said. "My husband worshipped your company. But he never thought he would die for some old man's insane dream."

"How could you do it?" Ron Jr. asked. "Deliberately set out to exterminate a sentient life form? It's..." He groped for the right word.

"Immoral?" I suggested.

"Incredible," Ron Jr. said. "Just incredible. The SA could shut us down for this, shut down the whole company."

"I own the SA," Spooner said. "Don't you worry about them. I can do whatever the hell I like out here. Always have and always will."

"You're behind the times, Dad," Ron Jr. said. "When did you last take a look at our public image surveys?"

"I don't give a fuck about our public image surveys..." Spooner began, but I hastily cut in on this
father-son brawl.

"All the same," I said, "this is what we've been
looking for for fifty years. A sentient lifeform, it's an
incredible find. Surely you can see that?"

"I've been looking for land, sonny," Spooner said.
"Wide open spaces. I never wanted any aliens clutter-
ing things up. Don't tell me what I've been looking for.
And you call this thing here sentient? A dog is more
sentient—at least you can train it not to bite your hand
off, or your prick. I'm talking metaphorically, you
understand."

"Oh, yes," Theron said. "We understand."

"Animal," Spooner said. "It's not even that, really,
but it thinks like an animal, all it knows is fucking and
killing. What if it is sentient? What are we going to do,
invite it to a tea party? It's in our way."

"You couldn't stand it," I said. "What she did to
you. She made you want to give it up, give it all up.
You, R. G. Spooner. She made you want to just let go
and sink right down into her, lose yourself completely."

"She's in our way," Spooner said again. "That's
all. An obstacle to be removed, no more than that.
There's nothing personal going on here."

"Forget it, Lewin," Theron said. "He doesn't want
to know. I don't think he could stand it if he did."

"It doesn't matter," McKinley said. "Doesn't
matter what he feels. Because she loves him, you see.
She has all along. And now that he's come back to her,
she's never going to let him go."

Heads turned to McKinley. She had moved away from Vichevski and now stood with her back to the wall. She was holding a laser pistol in her hand and it was pointing directly at R. G. Spooner.

45

"Tell your men to drop their weapons," McKinley said.

"I won't," Spooner said, in a rather uncertain show of bravado. "You're not going to kill me."

"She killed Muller," I reminded him. "And Duggan. I think she would."

He considered.

"Alright," he said, nodding to his men. They threw their weapons to the floor.

"We should never have come here," McKinley said, and I noticed that there was something strange about her voice. It seemed drained of all normal inflection. "Never ever. Should never have left Earth. I knew we had to stop it. Even before I came here, I knew it was wrong. Violating the universe."

"Looks like you hired yourself a Contractionist," Spooner told his son.

"I was a Contractionist, yes. We had a cell at Spooner U. I used to think that was very funny. But I never worked for your son. It was convenient to let him think I did, convenient to get him to arrange to send me here. This was the one project we wanted to stop most of all, and he wanted to stop it too. Not for the same reason of course, but what did that matter?''

"I never told you to kill anyone," Ron Jr. said. "Just to disrupt things a little. I thought that was what you had been doing here."

"Only a little, yes. Release those hallucinogens you gave me into the station, stir up rumors, help tip my husband over the edge. I never had to do much of that. I never used the drugs at all. I did start an affair with Arthur Duggan to drive Norm a little crazy. And I did work on Arthur, suggesting to him that strange things were happening here, things I couldn't account for: food disappearing from the galley, objects moving around in the night, shapes lurking outside in the mist.

"And it seemed to work. Because Arthur started to go... weird. He told me about his dreams. I thought I had made him dream them. I encouraged him to believe that there was something out there, calling him.

"And then one day I was in his room...we had just made love...that was about the only thing Arthur ever wanted to do at the end, I suppose it was the dreams that did it. We must have dozed off for a moment. When I woke up, I saw him leaving the room. Naked, he was sleepwalking, just like you did, only he really was naked. I got dressed and I followed him. I found him in the airlock. He hadn't even shut the inner door. He kept punching the exit button and the door kept saying, over and over, *'Inner door remains open. Further, sensors indicate that you are inadequately protected . . .*

"So I backed out of there and I closed the inner door. And then I went to the control room and I let him out."

"I never wanted you to kill anyone," Ron Jr. said.

"I already told you, I didn't kill him," she said. "I just helped him do what he wanted to do. But in any case, I wasn't working for you. I didn't have any reservations about killing people if it came to it, if it was necessary to shut down this station. It was only fair, after all, because we were killing this planet. At the time, of course, I didn't know how right I was about that."

"And then you drove Norm crazy," I said.

"I didn't have to," she said. "He did it to himself, mostly...that was what I thought. In fact I had to try to calm him down, once he started raving about seeing Arthur's ghost out there. He would have got himself recalled to Earth, and me with him, before I was finished here. And he did quiet down for awhile. But then he made more trouble for me."

"He started digging into Duggan's death," I said.

"I tried to discourage him, of course, but he became obsessed with it. He went to Franz, telling him about the safety program that should have stopped Arthur. And Franz looked into it and he realized that Norm was right. There was something there, even if it was just a mechanical failure, and he felt he really ought to file an addition to his original report on the death.

"Obviously, I didn't want him to do that. I didn't want any security people poking around down here. So I worked on Franz. I told him there was no need to report it. He would just get himself reprimanded for poor procedural work and that would be the end of the matter, because it was still a suicide after all. And in the end he agreed with me."

"You're lying," Vichevski said. "Franz was far too conscientious to do such a thing."

"At one time, perhaps. But you see, I think he was afraid it was Theron who had killed Arthur Duggan. And he wanted to protect her."

"Because he was having an affair with her?" I asked.

"That's not true," Theron said. "We were never lovers."

"I don't know whether they were or they weren't," McKinley said. "Knowing Franz, I would say not. He was a great believer in loyalty and duty and the sanctity of contracts. Yet I'm sure he wanted to be lovers."

"I don't understand," Theron said. "Why would he think that I killed Arthur?"

"Because I put that idea in his mind, without his realizing where it had come from. The same way I got Lewin to think you were the saboteur."

"So you took care of Muller," I said. "And then I showed up."

"Yes. I realized immediately that you had to be some kind of investigator. Certainly you were no leisure officer. My good friend Ronnie here was kind enough to confirm that for me. Then Norm got you asking questions again about Duggan's death. So I decided to keep you confused. You confused quite easily."

"Why?" I asked. "What could that gain you?"

"Time," she said. "Time for Gehenna to finish her work. You see, by this point I knew what was really going on here. I hadn't made Norm crazy, I wasn't disturbing your dreams—I hadn't done any of these things. Gehenna was doing it for me. I didn't have to do anything more to help shut down this station."

"But you did," I said. "You killed Muller and you wrecked the machines."

"In the end there was no other choice. The machines were killing us."

"Us?" Ron Jr. asked. "The machines were killing the Contractionists?"

"I said I was a Contractionist, but that's all over now. It's much too late for any of that. Now I'm . . . Gehenna."

"What?" Ron Jr. asked. "Run that one by me again."

"I am Gehenna," McKinley said. "She came to me, at last, in my own dreams, to gather me to her. And when my job is over, I will join her as Arthur joined her. But already I am a part of her."

"She's deluded," Ron Jr. said. "She thinks she's become an entire freaking planet. Talk about paranoid fantasy."

"Maybe she is deluded and maybe she isn't," I said. "But she's the one holding the laser pistol."

"You woke me," McKinley said, looking at R. G. Spooner, "from endless sleep. And then you left. But I waited. I knew you would return.

"And then the ships came with their bombs. The pain was terrible. And then came the cold. And then these stations, gouged from my body, spouting their poisons. Yet I survived, I . . . changed.''

"We stimulated something," I said, "by our very presence here. Sparked off some very rapid process of adaptation."

"The genetic change," Theron said. "Almost as if it absorbed Arthur. No doubt it wanted Remus, too. And you."

"Raw material," I said, feeling a thrill of fear.

"Love," McKinley said.

"We have to get out of this place," I said. "It's not just a moral issue, of whether we have any right to be here. We've got to get out of here while we still can."

"You can't leave now," McKinley said. "It's too late for that. Gehenna wants you, she wants all of you. Him first." She waved the gun at Spooner senior. "She's waited a long time for him."

She moved now to within a meter of Spooner, still pointing the gun at his head.

"Let's go, old man," she said. "We're going to take a little walk."

Spooner took a tentative step toward the door.

"No," I said. "Don't take him. I want to go first."

I moved, very slowly, toward her. The gun wavered between me and Spooner, finally settling on me.

"She wants me, too," I said. "More than him, maybe."

I took another step. Behind McKinley, I could see Spooner's bodyguards tense themselves for action.

"You're not going to shoot me," I told her. "She wouldn't like that at all. She loves me, after all. You must know that."

The bodyguards had picked up their weapons now. But they had no clear shot at McKinley. Spooner was in their line of fire.

"We'll go out together," I said. "Just the two of us. You can fix the lock for us, the way you did it for Duggan."

McKinley seemed confused. She continued to point the laser at me, but her grip seemed to waver.

"Just the two of us," I said. "She doesn't want the others. Just us. Can't you hear her calling us?"

And indeed, the voices were back now, inside my head, calling to me softly, crooning to me.

"Mother," McKinley said.

"Of course," I said. "Of course it is."

I was only a pace away from her now. The laser was pointed directly at my chest. Slowly, carefully, I reached out my hand to her.

"Give me your hand," I said. "We'll go out together. Out to play in the lovely white moss."

Still holding the pistol, she reached out her left hand toward me, turning slightly as she did so.

One of the bodyguards brought down R. G. Spooner to the floor in a flying tackle. The second discharged his weapon. A tiny hole opened up in McKinley's forehead, like a third eye. Her hand closed on mine, then let go. She fell to the floor at my feet.

The bodyguard who had shot her crossed the room and scooped up her laser from the floor, putting it in his pocket.

"You didn't have to do that," I told him.

"Of course he did," Spooner said, sitting up on the floor. "Of course he did. Nice work, boys." He climbed unsteadily to his feet. "Especially you, Lewin. You really had her going there for a moment. I could almost believe you really wanted to go out there with her."

"That's because I did."

46

Ron Jr. shook his head, as if to clear it.

"This is crazy," he said. "This is all crazy. I don't believe this, I don't believe any of it. I don't even want to think about it. I just want to get the hell out of here."

"Back to your desk?" his father asked. "Back to your big desk in your big office with the big windows? Back to your little games?"

"I'm a manager," Ron Jr. said. "I never pretended to be anything else. I never was interested in this space stuff. I've got people to do all that for me. So, yes, I want to go home. Now."

His father considered.

"Alright," he said. "There isn't much more we can do here for the moment. We should go back and regroup, make new plans, figure out a new line of attack."

"Attack?" Ron Jr. asked. "What are you talking about?"

"I'm talking about figuring out how to finish up this program here. Because I'm going to finish it, no question about that."

"What are you talking about?" Ron Jr. asked again. "How could you even think about continuing with this, after everything that has happened here?"

"We could develop some kind of weed-killer, maybe," the old man said thoughtfully. "Or maybe it's just a matter of using more nukes, kicking up a bunch more dust, cooling things down some more. Probably we should have used a bigger payload in the first place but the SA started to whine about it. I want to think about this some more, but right now I think that's our best plan. We can nuke selectively, keeping the stations intact for when we want to come back. And when the temperature goes down far enough, everything will die eventually. Oh, we'll be back, one way or another."

"You've got to be kidding," Ron Jr. told him. "We'll be lucky if we still have a company to run, once the SA hears about this. And Gehenna is going to be off-limits for sure."

"You think I don't know how to handle the SA, after all these years? And what will they hear, anyway? We'll tell them we had an accident here, that's all, an explosion in the machinery, a terrible tragedy which claimed the station commander and the food lady here. That's what happened. No one is going to tell them anything different."

"I am," Vichevski said promptly, and Theron and I nodded our heads in agreement. "We all will. We'll go to the SA together and put an end to this madness."

"You think they'll listen to you?" Spooner asked.

"Dad," Ron Jr. said, "once these people get to the SA, we're dead. You can't get away with this sort of stuff anymore. Forget it, don't even think about it."

"Perhaps you're right, Ronnie," Spooner said. "Perhaps I don't want to take a chance on that."

"Right," Ron Jr. nodded his head vigorously. "Now you're making sense."

"I changed my mind," Spooner said. "These people won't be going to the SA. They won't be going anywhere, don't worry about that."

"What are you going to do, try and buy us off?" Vichevski asked. "You can't buy me."

"Don't have to," Spooner told her. "You see, it looks like we had a bigger explosion here than I originally thought. Looks like we lost the whole crew."

"You're threatening us?" Theron asked.

"I'm not threatening you. I'm telling you why you're not coming back to Earth, why you won't be going to the SA. Reason is, you're dead. You're dead, ladies and gentleman, and you won't be talking to anyone about anything."

"You're going to have your goons kill us?"

"Not necessary," he said. "I'll just leave you here. Your communications are gone anyway, and there won't be anyone coming back here, not for quite awhile, not until we finish nuking."

"You're insane," Vichevski said.

"I've been called that before. It didn't bother me then, it doesn't bother me now. They were wrong then, you're wrong now."

"What about me?" Ron Jr. asked.

"What about you, Ronnie boy?"

"What are you going to do about me? Because if you leave these people here and try to go on with this program, I'm going to have to go to the SA instead of them. And don't call me 'Ronnie boy.' I don't like it."

Ron Jr. seemed surprised by his own show of resistance.

"Well, good for you, Ronnie," the old man said. "Good for you. Time you stood up to me instead of sneaking around behind my back. But the fact is, if I have to leave you here too, I will."

Ron Jr. stared into his father's eyes for a moment.

"You would, too," he said. "You'd rather leave me here than give up this craziness."

"Lose a hand, lose a son, what's the difference? You never were much of a son to me, anyway. Give me your word that you'll back me up on this and you can come home with me. Otherwise you stay here with them."

"You can't hope to get away with this," Ron Jr. said. "My people back on Earth..."

"You got no people, Ronnie. They're mine—they're all mine. I've got away with a helluva lot in my time, and I expect to get away with this, too. But if not, at least I gave it my best shot. Don't you see, I've got to finish this, finish what I started here? You can't expect me to stop now. So what's it gonna be?"

"No," Ron Jr. said. "I'm not going to make you any promises. No."

"Alright," the old man said. He motioned to his bodyguards.

"We're leaving," he said. "If you change your mind, Ronnie, you can still come with us. The rest stay here."

We watched as Spooner strode out of the room, followed by his bodyguards. Ron Jr. stood staring after them.

"Give him your word," I told him. "What does it matter? Stop grandstanding. Give him your word and go up to the ship, and the first chance you get, break it. It's our only shot."

"He'll think he won," Ron Jr. said. "He'll think he beat me again."

"What difference does it make? He's insane, after all. What possible difference does it make what he thinks of you?"

"Alright," he said, finally. "If that's how it has to be."

But Ron Jr. had agonized a little too long. As we came into sight of the main lock, we saw Spooner and his henchmen, now fully suited up, enter the passageway leading through to the vehicle bay. At the end of that passageway I could see their landing vehicle, parked beside the groundcars and flyers. As we reached the inner door, the door at the other end swung closed behind them.

I went to the portal and looked out into the bay, while Ron Jr. began clumsily to pull on his suit.

"Hurry," I said. "They're almost at the lander."

And then Gehenna herself erupted into the vehicle bay.

47

Afterward when I tried to reconstruct what occurred, I could no longer be sure about it. Yet it seemed to me that old man Spooner took a tentative step toward the outer vehicle door even before it burst open to unleash its furies.

Perhaps he saw it bulging inward and wanted to get a closer look at this strange phenomenon. Or perhaps, at the very last, he sensed and chose to embrace the destiny that he had so narrowly eluded before.

It was impossible to account for it, really, that freak combination of accelerated plant growth combined with high winds that must have piled moss up against the walls of the station, up and up, until finally it burst its way through those heavily reinforced doors. Impossible to account for it, that is, unless you were prepared to accept that it was quite deliberate.

It was surely not that Gehenna wanted to save us. She did it because she would not be denied the old man again, denied the one whose touch had once brought her so magically to life.

Spooner's henchmen, seeing the great tidal wave of moss rising upon them, at least tried to save themselves, turning to run before finally being overwhelmed. Spooner himself stood quite still, arms open wide, to await it.

Up to his shoulders in that sea of white, he seemed to stagger. And then we watched him disappear completely under the moss.

White mists rushed in through the broken door, obscuring the scene completely.

"My father...." Ron Jr. said.

"They were suited up," Theron said. "They should still be alive under there, although of course it can't be very pleasant."

She crossed to one of the control boards and began to flip some switches.

"Oxygen," she said. "The moss won't like it at all."

As new oxygen rushed into the vehicle bay to mingle with the outside air, the moss began to blacken and shrivel, seeming almost to writhe in agony.

Finally it was all dead, and shrunken enough that the outlines of the men in their bulky atmosphere suits began to appear. After awhile one of them stood up and began to look around in a dazed sort of way. He was, I realized later, the one who had shot McKinley.

"We should all suit up," Theron said, "and get out of here."

We walked out through the lock onto that carpet of dead moss. The man who had shot McKinley was kneeling over R. G. Spooner, or what had once been R. G. Spooner.

Spooner's faceplate was open. There was dead moss all over his face and in the cavities that had once been his eyes.

"Must have triggered the release mechanism," Theron said. I wasn't sure whether she was referring to the moss or to Spooner.

We went to help the second bodyguard. He was alive but in shock, a shock he did not recover from in the course of the entire voyage home, and, to my knowledge, ever.

I looked back. Ron Jr. was trying to drag his father's body toward the landing vehicle.

"Leave him here," I said. "It's going to be crowded enough. Let Gehenna have him."

We got into the lander, and we left Station Gehenna behind us.

"Maybe," Ron Jr. said, staring back at the murky white face of the planet receding below, "I should finish the job for him, complete the program. He would have wanted me to."

"Perhaps he would," I said. "But is that any good reason to do so?"

"No," he said, finally. "I don't suppose it is."

Ron Jr., I thought, was not made of the same stuff as his father, and that was just as well.

48

Ron Jr. never did become chief executive officer of R. G. Spooner Interplanetary Development Corporation. He resigned from the company at the request of the board of directors. He told the business press that he was planning to raise sheep in Australia. Perhaps he was joking, yet it seemed a fitting enough profession for a former head of human resources.

The Space Administration declared Gehenna permanently off-limits. It also exacted a heavy fine upon the company, although many said it was not heavy enough.

My shares in the company's pension plan nosedived, but had recovered modestly by the time I cashed them in to take a teaching position in a junior college in Arkansas. It paid about a third of my former salary with the company, and less even than my previous teaching job. Academically, it was a step backward from my old university position. But it was the best I could find, and it was a long way from Station Gehenna.

The company was sorry to see me go and offered a number of senior desk jobs with no requirement for further space travel, but my vertigo was too great even for these.

I have not kept track of Greta Vichevski, although I know that she resigned also, and I like to think she went to a more fulfilling medical practice.

Valerie Theron, of course, has become rich from her chain of franchised dream parlors. Often, when Jesse comes home to stay with me on his vacations, we take in a dream. He knows, however, that I do not watch the space dreams. Those dreams I can get at home.

Gehenna calls to me still, every now and then, across the vastness of space. She calls to me, but I do not listen. I get up out of bed and I take a beer from the fridge and I sit out on the porch and look at my garden, at the greens and browns and reds. I do not think of the whiteness. I do not think of it at all. Or at least, only from time to time.

Chilling novels of international espionage, intrigue and suspense

Chilling novels of international espionage, intrigue and suspense

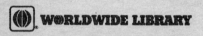